For Tokitae

Nateli Sanderson

Copyright © 2024 Nateli Sanderson

All rights reserved.

No part of this book may be used, reproduced, or transmitted in any manner without expressed written consent of author.

Dedicated to my Mom and Dad,
and my dog, Miley Anna

-

And to everyone who cares about animals
and the environment. You inspire me daily.

Prologue

With every step, the sand and little pebbles feel warm under my bare feet. I feel the calm wind pushing the salty air through my lungs and hear the sound of the waves delicately brushing up against the shoreline, a sense of peace filling me. The sky is painted in beautiful pinks and oranges with the backdrop of darkening blue.

Taking a deep breath, I lower the cedar branch in the water, and as I watch it being carried off to sea, I think of her. I get this heavy sinking feeling in the pit of my stomach. I miss her. It shouldn't have ended like this.

I wade out ankle-deep into the ocean, taking in the solitude of the evening. Despite everything, I am grateful for her. As I lay out the next cedar branch, I think, "Thank you."

As the world starts to darken into night, I

For Tokitae

watch those cedar branches disappear, feeling content, knowing that she's here with me. Knowing there is hope.

For Tokitae

Chapter One
Cordelia

The ocean pulls me in, and that is what I become. The warm, spring breeze catches me like a fire. My gaze does not leave the ocean as I wait anxiously, watching carefully, hoping that a whale will surface at any moment.

I look at the clock on my phone to see that I've been sitting here in the same spot on the rocky shoreline for about an hour. I stand up, and my legs begin to ache from sitting in the same position for so long. I stretch out and head to the little lighthouse.

"Hi Corey! I'm guessing you want to know if we've had any sightings today?" Janice asks as she looks down at me from under her rectangle-shaped glasses.

"Of course she's here for the orcas! What

else would it be?" Ed exclaims with a smile.

I nod.

"Well, you're in luck, kiddo. J pod is heading North and are coming down to us," she says as she flashes a smile of her crooked teeth.

I return the smile and say, "Thanks."

Janice and Ed are researchers here at the lighthouse, I've known them since I was a little girl. They're like family to me.

I rub my thumb over a smooth rock that I found here the very first time I came, and I look around the familiar little lighthouse feeling at home.

My eyes dance across the room of the cramped but familiar little building. The walls are covered with data and pictures of whales and marine life encounters. There's a counter where the researchers work, and behind the counter is even more data and pictures of whales. But I don't have time to stay and hang out at the lighthouse, the Js are coming!

I feel the cold metal bar under my arms as I push the heavy doors open and walk out. The light, fresh spring air fills my lungs, and an ocean

For Tokitae

breeze catches my hair. I perch myself on a jagged moss-covered rock that overlooks the vast expanse of the Salish Sea.

I become aware of everything, the rocky surface under me, the swaying of the long grass in the calm winds, and the texture of the salty air. I shut my eyes, fading into it, in hopes of becoming more than I am. Before I know it, they're here.

Excitement rushes through me, bubbling out of me as I see them approach. There's not any feeling in the entire world quite like this one. It's the sound of the majestic beast surfacing and exhaling sharply that gets to me. It makes a shiver of excitement go up my spine as I open my eyes to see the open ocean. I scan the water to see the figures surfacing and diving back down under the blanket of water again off in the distance. They're coming from the south and heading north to hunt.

Soon enough they're swimming right past me making beautiful sounds as they exhale through their blowholes. There must be about twenty of them, swimming closely as they hunt and play. I notice that Slick J16 is in the front, you can see her unique saddle patch as she porpoises. Sticking close to her side is, of course, her son, Mike J26. Just before my eyes, I see him jump up, flinging his body into the air freely, and hear him slap against the water.

Shachi J19 swims up on her side by the surface, she lifts her tail out of the water, and slams it down against the surface. Making a loud crashing sound that echoes in my mind.

I'm lucky to live in the Salish Sea. Around here, we have our very own population of orcas: The Southern Resident Orcas. They diet on salmon, specifically the Chinook. The SRKW (Southern Resident Killer Whales) population is made up of three pods: the J, K, and L pods. Pods are groups of orcas that travel together - they're like one big family, each pod has their own dialect and hunting strategies. They are a big part of my life and are *the* icon for the Pacific Northwest. Many people, including myself, know them by name. Because they are an apex predator, when they struggle, it's a realization that our whole ecosystem is not healthy.

Unfortunately, there are only 73 left… they need our help fast…

Before I know it, the Js disappear. As quickly and quietly as they came, they fade back into the open ocean, chasing the sunset.

I wish that I could fade into the sunset, too. I wish that it would bring me with it and take me into the solitude of the night. I would walk among the stars and then return with the early sunrise.

But of course, that's simply not going to happen, so, I reluctantly hop onto my bike and pedal down the road. The little grayish house with black trimming comes into sight. I sigh as I feel the cold metal doorknob prickle my fingertips. I slowly open the door trying to be as quiet as possible, and creep in.

The floorboards creak as I walk down the stairs and into my bedroom in the basement. I slowly let go of the door handle, so it silently closes. I strip off my jeans, replace them with shorts, and pull my boxy t-shirt over my head. I creep into the bathroom across the hall and take my toothbrush and paste out of the drawer. I stare emptily at my reflection, my bright green eyes staring right back at me. My long, wavy, autumn-brown hair falls in front of my face. I try to brush through it, but that only makes it frizzier, of course. I sigh and stare at the ceiling out of boredom. Suddenly, I hear yelling coming from upstairs.

My parents... of course.

I make a beeline back to my bedroom and slam the door behind me. I sink to the floor.

Why can't they just get along?

I pull out my smooth stone from Lime Kiln and brush my thumb along it nervously. *Just don't think about anything* I tell myself, as I focus on the rock.

My heart starts to race and I tense up as the yelling turns into screaming back and forth. I can hear my dad yelling a string of cuss words and my mom sobbing and saying things I can't make out from downstairs. I don't know when they'll stop. It's gone on for hours before. I can't not think about it, it spreads like a disease infecting my mind.

The thing is, I live in Friday Harbor,

Washington. Here, all the houses seem to be perfect and fancy, including ours… or at least on the outside. But on the inside, it's a tangled web of fights, yelling, and lies that's breaking us all down slowly. I'm a fly stuck in this spider's web and there's no way out.

That night I lie awake staring at the ceiling. The lingering silence and the stillness of the night hit me, there's nothing to distract me now from my own thoughts. It gets tedious after a while.

Being fifteen in today's world kind of sucks. Right when you feel like you understand it all, you realize you know nothing at all. Then there's this broken up world that we are being left with, and you want to make an impact, but you don't know how, and you feel too hopeless to even try. We've been told about issues like social injustices and climate change. We've been told that we "haven't seen nothing yet." But what does that all mean? What can I do about it? Nothing. It's hard to come to terms with the future that has been compromised for us.

If only I had known back then what I know

now. That would've made things much easier. This is the story of how I found hope, how I started to change things, how I found myself.

This is the story of Cordelia Hart.

Chapter Two
Lolita

The water hits me and splashes up with a thunderous roar. My trainer has a big grin on his face because I followed his meaningless instructions.

I look into his icy blue-gray eyes, wondering if this means anything more than just his greed. Then I remind myself, I shouldn't be so harsh on these humans. If it didn't mean anything to any of my trainers, they would've chosen a different livelihood. They must care… just not enough to think about what's best for me.

"Good job today, Lolita! Can we breach one more time?" he says enthusiastically. I don't know why they keep calling me that. I *hate* it. It's like a mask that I'm being forced to wear.

For Tokitae

I turn sharply and swim as fast as I can without running into any walls in this cramped little prison. Then I launch myself out of the water. Flying through the air, I feel as free as I have in a long time. I guess that's all I have now, my little freedoms. I must hold on to those moments. They are *mine* and they can't be bought.

"Lolita!" he shouts as he rubs the water from his eyes. Oops… I guess I accidentally splashed him with that last breach. He should be glad though, the water is cooler than the air, and it must have been refreshing. I saved him from the scorching spring Miami heat.

"Do you want the salmon?" he taunts. I am hungry, and even though the salmon tastes different then at home, I want that salmon, so I must do the trick without splashing him.

I remember the pride I felt the first time I had caught a salmon all by myself. The texture of the scales on my tongue, the rusty taste of its blood, and the acceptance I felt among my family and our home. Salmon used to be my favorite treat in the world, especially the

Chinook. Now I dread eating them, although I can't imagine eating anything else.

I miss hunting. We would all pitch in, and we would all talk and signal to each other when there were salmon. We spent our days hunting and playing. Some days, we would swim over a hundred miles! Salmon were scarce, so many times we were hungry. I guess that's one thing I don't miss… the hunger. I loved playing with my pod. I remember the joy and freedom I felt as we breached, and spy-hopped and swam fast. I miss those days… they sure didn't last long.

I swim to the northernmost end of my tiny tank - which doesn't take me long because it's so small compared to me - and then I swim forward, jump up, and boop my nose to the tip of the stick.

"Good job! You're gonna do so great at the show!" he congratulates me. At least he talks to me. Even though I can't talk back, it's still nice to be talked at. There is a constant monotonous silence in my mind, so being talked at – even meaninglessly - still kind of interrupts that silence, but doesn't quite satisfy me.

I don't hear any other commands from the trainers, so I poke my head above the water to see what's going on.

"She's tricky today, really stubborn," he says to the woman trainer.

"Let me try, I think she likes me," she says. I like her as much as one can possibly like a human being.

"Hey, Lolita! How are you today? I hear it's not a good day? We're gonna make it a good day, okay? Are you ready?" she talks to me in this high-pitched voice like I've seen their kind talking to their young. I don't like it. I turn away, but I don't splash her.

"Oh, please! You know you can't do this in a show!" she begs. I turn around and swim right up to where she is sitting and look her dead in her big, brown eyes. Fine, I'll do what she wants.

I just hope that one day, someone will see me, and care enough to get me out of this imprisonment. That, I suppose, is my only hope. I need to get good at shows and maybe that will be.

Maybe it's not so bad. I've lived here for

over fifty years now. I miss having other orca companions, but maybe it's not *that* bad. I still feel bitter about the whole situation, but at least I am being taken care of. I do think maybe these people might care at least a little bit.

    I guess I just have to make the best of it. Or at least that's what I tell myself...

For Tokitae

Chapter 3
Cordelia

I stare at the clock; 2:27. In only a few minutes I will be free, but for now, I am sitting alone, only half-listening to the teacher's math lesson. I tap my pencil lightly against my desk, counting the seconds in my head.

Yet as it always does, time slips away; the minutes turn into seconds, and before I know it, I'm heading to Lime Kiln as I always do after school.

A light drizzle mists against my face, and fog sets in near the treetops. I put force on the pedals of my bike as I boundlessly speed up, bracing against the harsh winds. As I approach Lime Kiln, I ditch my bike in the parking lot and rush down the trail directly to the lighthouse. The rain and the wind become monstrous as they unsettle the sea.

I walk down to the lighthouse and find Mrs. Miller bent over a computer.

"No sightings today?" I ask.

"Nope. Sorry, sweetheart. All pods are up in Canadian water. We haven't seen any whales at all today," she replies.

I shrug. "Alright, thanks… When's the next Ferry to Canada?" I joke.

She laughs and pushes her gray-white hair away from her face.

"Well, I guess I'll be on my way! Thanks!" I say as I turn to leave.

"Bye!" she calls after me.

Soon enough I get home to see that both of my parents' cars are in the driveway. And when I open the door, I hear yelling, which isn't really a surprise anymore.

"I'm home!" I yell carelessly as I swing the door closed.

I wait a second for a response, but the only response I get is the displeasing sharpness of silence. I shrug and stomp down to my bedroom. The fighting continues, and I get overwhelmed;

I've really had enough. I slam my door shut and crawl up onto the top of my bed, not bothering to get under the covers. I can still hear the muffled shouting even when I cover my ears.

Eventually it dies down. I bury my wet face into my pillow and try to take deep breaths to calm myself down.

It feels like something inside me just sinks, and I know the fighting will soon return. I sit up and look around my room. My plain white walls are covered with pictures I've taken when I watch whales or artwork that I've made, all from a long, long time ago.

Nowhere around my room do I have family pictures, and the only family picture that we do have is in the entryway hall. I remember that day very well; my parents paid someone to take a picture of us all together. We all were dressed in fine clothes: my dad in his dress pants and button-up shirt, my mom in her skin-tight red dress, and me in my earthy green dress that went down to my knees. That was the one time I had worn it and the one time I had dressed up nice. My hair was halfway pulled back into a braid, and my mom had a long thick braid that was wrapped around her head and into a bun in the back. All of us wore fake smiles.

To my surprise, my mom enters my room not long after the yelling stops. Her long eyelashes are wet with tears, her face red, her eyes watery, her lips parted and dry.

"Hi, Corey. I'm sorry about that," she says. Questions and caution fill her voice. She doesn't even know how to talk to me.

"It's fine," I say shortly.

"Do you want to know what that was about?" she asks.

"I don't know, do I?" I say as I side-eye her.

Tension fills the air as the silence attacks us, neither of us knowing what to do or say next, both of us afraid to hurt the other.

"Not really. I don't want to know," I say.

"That's fair. I just want you to know your dad is going away for a little bit. He's spending some time with Grandma and Grandpa. While he's gone, I want to take you to Miami with me. Do you want to go on a trip?" she explains.

She acts as if I'm supposed to just go along

with everything she says; I'm supposed to understand it all and not ask questions.

 I sigh, "Mom! You can't expect me to just leave without telling me a thing! Why even Miami? How long? When? How long is Dad gonna be away? Why isn't he coming with us? Why are we just suddenly taking a trip? We've never taken trips in the past, and you haven't even mentioned it! And where's Dad right now?" Maybe I shouldn't have said I didn't want to know because now my thoughts are flooded with questions.

 She sighs a long, tired, sad sigh. "I know, I know. I'm terrible to you. I don't know anything about you… I hardly know you. I'm sorry, you're right, I should probably answer some of your questions. So, I'll start from the beginning. Dad and I got into a fight and we need some time apart now… I don't know how long, or if we're ever going to be able to be together again.
But it wasn't supposed to be like this." Her words are cracked and broken and now there is a tear running down her cheek.

 "But I want to fix our life as much as we

can now. So, I need to get away from here… at least for a little while. I want to spend this trip getting to know you and getting away from your father. So, on Monday, two weeks from now, we'll head out and spend one week in Miami," she explains.

I try to talk but the words are dry and unable to come. I'm speechless. "That all sounds great, but what about school?"

"I mean, it's just one week, can't you do homework? You've never really missed much before, you deserve a break," she says.

"Well, I guess," and that is all I can say. I want to say more, but I have no words. I just don't know what's happening.

With that, my mom turns to leave. She closes the door behind her, and once again I am left alone.

Another day slips away and I'm back at Lime Kiln. It's a busy day, and I am being put to work by Mrs. Miller. The Ks, who don't come by here very often, were spotted down South and are supposed to be headed our way. Lots of people are stopping by, which is a little strange seeing as how it's a pretty cold day for the spring. But people are always eager to see the orcas. I don't blame them, I am, too. But they also have lots of questions, and the people who work here have to collect data, so it's my job today to answer any questions visitors have.

I stand outside of the lighthouse and stare out into the open ocean. A girl who looks like she's about my age walks up to me.

"Is it a guarantee that we'll see them?" she asks.

"Nope. Even though they're heading our way, they could still turn around at any time," I say.

"Oh…" her voice trails off.

"It's okay! We just need to be hopeful! Have you ever seen them before?" I ask. I change my tone to try to sound encouraging when I see how disappointed she is with my answer.

"Not in the wild. But I know Lolita very well, that's why I wanted to come down here. I wanted to see her family, and where she came from." She says as she pushes away her short dark brown hair from her brown-gold eyes.

"Who's Lolita?" I ask.

"You don't know? She's an orca from here but she lives in Miami at the aquarium my mom works for. I get to spend a lot of time with her because of my mom. And I'm so glad I do. She's the best," the girl explains with a smile.

"Really? I don't know how I didn't know that," I say. "Well, what brings you here? Just orcas?"

"We're at some family reunion. I hate having to talk to people I barely know, even though they know everything about me somehow… you know? They always say how grown-up I've become, which is so annoying because what am I supposed to say to that? I'm just glad about the whales," she explains. "I really hope I get to see them! That would make this trip totally worth it."

I just smile at that, not knowing what to say. I've never been to a family reunion before. I've met some of my closer family members, but never my distant cousins and people. I wonder if they'd know everything about me?

"I know what you mean," I lie. With a long pause, I add, "I hope you get to see the orcas. That's one of my favorite things about volunteering here - seeing all the people get so excited about them when they see them for the first time."

I don't think I was very helpful for Janice and Ed for the rest of the day; I wasn't really present, I was too busy thinking about Lolita, going to Miami and family reunions. Why does that make me sad, somehow? I've never really thought about the lack of extended family before.

For Tokitae

Chapter Four
Lolita

There's a crowd of people watching me with excitement shining in their wide smiles. I listen to the chatter of the people in the audience, and I see a few of them pointing at me and talking with excitement. The water vibrates, the beat drops and the melody carries on. My head starts to pound like the pounding in the music. Although my mind refuses, I have to do this. And yet, this is just another day in the life for me.

It's like what my friend, Hugo, told me when I was first brought here: I have to do their tricks to get salmon, and then I have to do their tricks in front of a larger group of people. Hugo was also captured from my family. Although he was brought into captivity before I was born so I never got to meet him in the wild. Unfortunately,

For Tokitae

after about twelve years, the suffering got to him. He bashed his head into the wall until it killed him.

I miss him tremendously, but I go on doing my shows. I stay strong, I do as I'm told day after day. It gets to my mind at times, but I hold on, for he was not able to.

The loud splash of the dolphins performing brings me back to today and I prepare myself for the show. It starts with the music, then the dolphins splashing in the water and jumping in unison. One of the woman trainers gives me some salmon, and that's when I know to come in with a breach.

I send a giant wave throughout the entire tank as I swim fast gaining speed. Then I launch myself into the air, my heart rate accelerating as I come back down with a giant splash. I love breaching, sometimes. While in mid-air, I close my eyes and imagine myself in the real ocean. That is my little freedom.

After getting another fish, I swim over to my trainer to let her climb on. Three of my trainers are doing the show with me. All three of them are throwing their arms around and swaying their long limbs to the beat of the loud, loud, music. As I approach the trainer with the fish, she stops swinging her arms and climbs onto me.

She almost pinches my flipper with her long fingers. I take her around a lap holding her up proudly, and then bring her back to the divider in the tank on which the trainers were standing.

I get another salmon, and then the trainer gets back up and starts dancing again, but now they expect me to dance with them. I twirl and twirl in unison with the trainers.

Next, I flop onto my back and float for a second.

Out of nowhere comes a loud booming voice. I can't make out the words over the loud crowd of people. I hear a few words like, "Miami Sea Aquarium," "1955," "white-sided dolphin," and "killer whale." I hate it when they call me a killer whale. I've killed no one. Sometimes I wonder, do *they blame me for Hugo's death? M*aybe that's why they're calling me a killer. But really, I haven't killed anyone, I'm just an orca, so why don't they simply call me an orca?

For Tokitae

Chapter Five
Cordelia

Two weeks pass in the blink of an eye. It hadn't seemed like any time had passed at all because everything happened so quickly. In the meantime, I hadn't seen my dad at all, and my mom was being oddly clingy. We had been busy planning our trip and packing, and these events brought us closer together. In elementary school, I remember them telling us to crumple up a piece of paper, then try to flatten out the wrinkles and creases. Will they ever go away fully? No. That's what happens when you break someone's trust: it can get better over time, but never goes away fully. That's the only way I know how to describe where my mom and I are at right now.

Today is the day that we are traveling to

Miami, and it's going to be a long day. It's about twelve forty-five, all my bags are packed and I'm ready to go. I shove the last bite of lunch in my mouth and head out the door.

We don't live in downtown Friday Harbor. So, it takes about fifteen-ish minutes to drive down the windy roads of the small island and finally get to the docks.

We're on a pretty small island, but I love living here. I love everything about it. Down by the docks, when you first get off the ferry, the streets are covered in little shops and restaurants; it's very touristy. But the rest of the island is very scenic without many people. I love driving and not passing another car for miles; it's just a very peaceful island.

Downtown gives off a very happy small-town vibe. Only two-thousand seven-hundred forty-seven people live on this tiny island. But downtown is crowded with many tourists in the summertime.

We still have about fifteen/twenty minutes until the ferry starts unloading and loading. We depart at one twenty-five. I step outside our little

For Tokitae

Volvo for a second to take in a deep breath of the salty air. I feel the comforting warmth of the sun shining down on me. The air smells fresh as it always does in early May. It's funny just how fast our weather changes in the spring. Just a couple of weeks ago, we surely got some April showers, and now, everything's green and fresh and happy. I just love the spring.

    The weather was even more enjoyable on the ferry. After we boarded and departed, Mom and I went out to the observation deck. I step up on the railing and lean over, mesmerized by the propellers spinning over and over. We leave a trail of white foamy bubbles, spreading out and evaporating, becoming the blueish-greenish color of the sea.

    Looking out onto the horizon I see us leave our home, watching our tiny island as it becomes smaller and smaller. The view changes fast as we pass more islands, different islands, all covered in the beautiful evergreen trees. I close my eyes to hear the gentle splashing of the boat and the water. I feel the warmth of the sun embrace me, and the texture of the fresh salty air fills me, taking me away. I drown in my surroundings, taking it all in.

I jump up on the railing holding to it tightly, and I feel the wind brush past me. I feel the pulse in my palm, and I feel alive. Not living, *alive*. I can't help the grin spreading across my face as I let out a little cheer.

"You excited?" my mom asks with a smile and a laugh.

"*Yes!* We've never really traveled before… of course, I'm excited!" I say.

"That's good. I'm just nervous. It feels weird just leaving your dad without even telling him," she says, her voice full of sorrow and doubt.

"What the heck? Why wouldn't you tell him?" I ask, starting to get a little frustrated.

"Our last fight was pretty bad, I didn't want to bother him again," she says.

"What if our plane crashes and we die? Dad won't even know that we had left in the first place!" I exclaim.

"Our plane won't crash, they never do. Just don't worry about it, sweetheart," she says.

I roll my eyes at her and storm off in a huff.

I get hit with the cool air from the inside of the ferry, which feels good because my face feels hot with anger.

I storm out of the halls with the tables, and find a new kind of dining area. There's a shelf full of pamphlets; I grab a whole bunch of random ones and sit down in an empty chair and start to look through them. Quite a few of the pamphlets are advertising for Friday Harbor. I look through one for the Whale Museum, and I try to identify some of the orcas that are pictured, but I can't. Some of the pictures only show a fluke or an orca skeleton, and obviously you can't identify them by that.

Out of the corner of my eye, I see my mom power walking over to me, running a hand through her wind-tossed hair.

"Corey! Calm down, it's okay. You need to learn how to manage your anger issues," she says shortly as she sits down next to me.

"Well, where do you think I get them? Hmm? It's not like I was surrounded by angry people all the time," I reply.

"I know. Well, if it makes you feel better, I texted your father," she says as she presses her lips tightly together. I know that look that she has; that look when she kind of stares off into space with her lips pressed tightly together. That is the same look she has every time she and Dad fight. Maybe I shouldn't be so hard on her... at least she's trying.

"It's okay, Mom. Thanks for taking me on this trip," I whisper.

The ferry pulls into the docks and we're off driving through Anacortes. Anacortes has a very different vibe than Friday Harbor. Even though it's still a pretty small town on the water, there are many, many more people and the streets are much busier. It feels so strange driving past so many cars, and we go so fast.

We spend at least another two hours on the road. It was a long two hours of staring out the window and thinking about how different it is here. Finally, we reach Seattle.

I can hear my heart pounding. Excitement pours over me, and I feel like I can't sit still. I want to hop out of the car and explore the huge city. At first glance, Seattle is filled with towering buildings with windows that shine like a new penny. The roads are filled with cars and trucks, bumper to bumper in about four lanes. I can't even count the number of cars I see.

All of the sudden the cars slow down and we are stuck sitting here trapped in a maze of cars and left to the torture of our boredom.

"Why aren't we going?" I ask.

"Ugh! I hate driving in the city! It's a slowdown, honey," my mom says in a frantic voice.

"When will we be able to go again? Will we be late to the airport?" I ask.

"Corey, I wish I knew the answer to both of those questions," she replies.

I roll down my window and stick my head out like a dog in need of some fresh air. I close my eyes and listen to the sounds of honking and cars in other lanes passing by. I take a deep breath but choke on the air in my lungs. I wasn't expecting it to smell like that. The air is different from home, instead of fresh and free, it is dirty and tight. It smells like gasoline and cigarettes.

My head starts to throb.

Once you look deeper, you see the tents of homeless camps on the streets and the garbage that litters everywhere. Once you look deeper, you see the problems that are so plain to see, yet no one bothers to fix them.

The traffic speeds back up, and within 20 minutes we arrive at the airport. Under the bright fluorescent lighting, people walk speedily from one place to another. Everyone has a destination, and everyone knows that there is a long process to get to that destination.

We have to sign in and my mom has to fill out paperwork and scan her card about ten times. Our luggage has to go through security, we have to go through security. We have to find a line to go through to get to our waiting area to get onto the correct plane. We have to get our bags to the correct location. It's stressful, exhausting, and exciting all at once.

After a little less than an hour, I finally sit down to see that it's almost five twenty. Now we have to sit and wait for our plane to return, unload its passengers, and load ourselves on.

Before I know it, I'm sitting down on the plane. On one side of me, my mom, with a magazine held delicately in her hands and on the other side of me, a little circle of a window.

I take deep breaths and try to calm myself; I'm scared of what's to come. I've never been on a plane before, I don't know what to expect. I hear a *ding* and a voice comes on through the speakers.

"Welcome aboard!"

For Tokitae

Chapter Six
Lolita

Yet another sunny day here in Miami. Yet another day filled with the same boring things. The first thing that I do is bob my head out of the water and look around. The paint looks like it is peeling even more on the empty stadiums. I hate it when the flakes of paint fall into my water and turn it gross-er than it already is.

　　I dive back down under the surface of the water and swim another lap around. It doesn't take long at all - my tank is tiny and crowded with the other dolphins. Because of lack of anything else to do, I try to dive down to the bottom of my tank and end up with my fluke out of the water. That's right, I can't dive because I'm longer than my tank is deep, and this is in the deepest part of the tank.

One of my trainers walks in and starts rummaging through the equipment. She tosses me a salmon as she greets me and starts to prepare me for practice. I like this trainer a bit more than the others. She keeps to herself for the most part, but is still friendly to me, and sometimes lets her children see me. I love them.

"What are you doing today?" her daughter asks as she walks around the corner. My day always gets a little bit better with her here.

"Just the same things as usual for today. Going through the routine for shows and things," the trainer replies.

"Can I say hi?" the girl asks eagerly.

"Yeah, go ahead, Ellie," her mom returns.

Ellie's already closer to me than most visitors are allowed to be. Slowly she approaches me, walking carefully on the beam that separates my tank. She sits down by the bucket of salmon. I swim up to her, bob my head out of the water, and stare at her blankly.

I'm not just doing this out of boredom, I like this girl. There's something different to her. She's old enough to the point where she's not like one of those little kids, wobbling around saying weird things in their weird voices. She's not that old either. She's not yet poisoned by this world, still new enough to be hopeful. I stare back into her wide brown eyes. Her expression is soft, and there's a spark of hope shining in those eyes that stare right back at me.

Her mom has worked here for quite a while now, and so I've watched her and her brother grow up. It's a strange feeling to see them grow and change; I've never really bonded with humans like I've bonded with them before.

"'Morning, Lolita!" she greets me as she passes me a fish.

I spin around in a circle with joy and pop my head up on the beam right beside her. She giggles and slowly rubs her hand on the top of my head, back and forth, gently.

"I swear you're her favorite person!" her mom calls out with a smile. "She doesn't act like that with anyone else."

She is one of my favorite people. I am grateful for some humans.

But I still miss my home, my family, my

freedom. I still remember what I learned from the wild. I will always carry it with me. It's all I have left - just the lessons I learned and the memories I made.

    I will never forget.

Chapter Seven
Cordelia

It's been almost six hours of horror, pure horror. I've decided that I hate flying. It feels so unnatural. I look out the window and see clouds and nothingness. I'm crammed into an uncomfortable seat next to my mom with some stranger on the other side of her. I'm ready to get off. *Please, please land soon!*

Lucky for me, I hear that comforting beep, meaning that there is going to be an announcement.

"Buckle your seat belts, and prepare for landing," a masculine voice says over the intercom.

I hear the sharp clicks of the seat belts all around me, and then I shut my eyes tight and silently promise myself that I'm not going to open them until the plane stops.

Before I know it, I'm stepping off the plane. As soon as I step out the door, a muggy heat strangles me. The air is very different than home. It's very humid and I don't think that I like it at all, but at the same time, the warmth is almost comforting.

I find myself standing in a busy airport with people frantically dashing around. Outside the huge glass window is a nice sunny day.

Our Uber comes to pick us up, and soon we're driving through the vibrant city. In a way, it kind of reminds me of Seattle. It has the same towering buildings and busy roads, but it's very different here. The many evergreen trees are replaced with palm trees reaching up towards the sky. The streets are much more colorful and the air smells like fancy foods with a mix of gasoline and cigarettes, just like Seattle.

Our hotel comes into sight, and the car begins to slow as we pull into the parking lot. As I walk through the sliding glass doors, the cool air hits me, and I immediately feel relaxed. I feel like there was a blanket wrapped around me, wrapped so tight that I was being strangled, and as I walk into the hotel, the blanket is finally coming off and I feel free again. The hotel isn't anything fancy, but it's nice, clean, fresh, and it has a swimming pool and free breakfast, so that's a win.

    The sun starts to set in the busy city. Even at night, the city is still awake. There are still loud cars speeding down the highways and bright lights that light up buildings. People are still out and about. My mind is still out and about, and I can't even close my eyes. I lie awake in the unfamiliar hotel bed and wait for time to pass. Eventually, I do start to drift off.

    The next morning, I wake up with the sun shining in our hotel window, casting a warm welcoming yellow glow across the room. I take in a deep breath of air and hop out of bed.

    Today we're going to see Lolita!

Chapter Eight
Lolita

"Would you like to try to work with her today?" the trainer asks her daughter. "I think she would listen to you well."

"You do?" Ellie asks, surprised. "But she thinks of me as like a friend, not a trainer."

"You know what she thinks now?" she asks sarcastically.

She groans, "I just wanna be her friend, not her trainer."

"Why don't you ask her," Mom suggests.

"Okay. Lolita, how would you like it if I trained with you today? Do you think it would be fun?" she asks me.

I spin around in circles and give her a big smile. She and I have this way of communicating even though we don't speak the same language.

"Yeah? You wanna work with me?" she asks again with excitement.

I nod.

"Well, I'll make sure to be the best trainer that you work with," she says as she holds her head up high with a grin on her face.

I've heard her mother call her Ellie many times before; a name that suits her, I think. She looks just like her mother, too. The same big, brown, kind eyes, olive skin, and straight dark brown hair that falls around their round faces.

She sits down on her knees and reaches out to me. I swim up to her and she gently pats my head and gives me a salmon. Her smile floods into her eyes, and she speaks to me in a hushed voice, "Don't tell Mom, but I thought you needed a salmon to start training with, too."

I return her smile. I wish I could talk back to her. I wish we could have a *real* conversation.

"Well, now we have to start your training. I'm sorry, Lolita, I wish I could give you a day of *peace!*" she groans. It's funny that she says that though, because I like training, it gives me something to do at least.

So, we go do just that. A lot of the practice she can't do with me though because she's not my trainer. The only thing is hand signals and that sort of thing; getting me to breach, raise one of my flippers, spy hop and dive.

Pretty soon, her mom steps in. "Okay, I've got to take over from here."

Chapter Nine
Cordelia

It's about ten thirty in the morning now. I feel wide awake with the rambunctious noises of my surroundings. We've arrived at the aquarium! Crowds of excited people walk by under the beating sun. Everyone is dressed for the weather in t-shirts, shorts, and baseball caps.

I walk through the gates, side-by-side with my mom, following the crowd. The first thing I see is the crowded gift shop with people coming in and out of it. Mom walks down to a nearby bench and sits down. I follow.

"Where do we want to go?" she asks as we look down at the map we got when we first entered.

I smirk, "Hmm... I wonder where I would want to go? What would I want to do?"

She returns my smirk. "Yeah, I don't know. That's why I asked you." Silence lingered in the air for a second or two before she spoke again. "How about we keep walking and look at the other animal exhibits first before going to see Lolita?"

"Alright," I agree.

First stop, the flamingo exhibit. Although kept behind a fence, these beautiful light pink and white birds are still free-range. They look very content as they stand there; still, blank, peaceful, and happy.

After watching the flamingos for a bit, we slowly drift away. There's this building - on the outside, it's white and almost a circle-like shape, with a big sign that reads: Sea Aquarium. When we walk in, I get reminded of that feeling I felt when going into the hotel, like the weight of the humid air was being removed.

"Where are we now?" I ask my mom.

"The dolphin lobby," she replies.

The strong scent of fresh food and pretzels hits us as we walk past the snack place. Again, I see another gift shop. I think this one is specific to the dolphin lobby. Lots of families walk by hand-in-hand, taking in the fun of the aquarium and the dolphins.

The space is open, but there's a lot of people so it makes it seem a lot smaller than it actually is. The dimly lit, blue-toned lighting reflects off everything: people's smiling faces as they walk by, the shiny clean ground, the walls, the glass of the dolphin exhibit.

I grab my mom's arm and pull her over to the dolphins. We stand with three bottlenose dolphins splashing and playing around us, the only barrier between us is the glass. They look so smiley and happy, yet mischievous, as they glide through the water. It's almost as if they're showing off, swimming so close to the glass, saying, "Look at me, and my beauty!"

Little kids run towards them, putting their hands and little faces up against the cold glass.

With wide excited eyes, and an ear-to-ear grin, a little kid exclaims, "Mommy! The dolphin looked at me! I'm the king of animals!"

His mom crouches down to his level to get a better look at the dolphins. The baby in her arms points at the dolphins in awe, and then brings her hand back to hold the binky in her mouth.

One dolphin swims up close to the glass, twisting and turning in the water. The light dancing on the surface reflects on its pale skin as it dives.

"Look at how cute they are!" my mom exclaims.

"They really are. Look at their smiles," I respond.

"I think Lolita is over on the other side of this building. Do you want to go see her now?" she asks.

"Nah… I'm good," I joke.

"That's what I thought," she replies as we turn around to leave the same way that we entered. The air clings to us again as we walk. I'm already regretting wearing jeans. Among the chatter of all the tourists, you can hear some of them talking about Lolita.

"Are you excited to see the killer whale?" a pregnant woman in front of us asks the little girl that she's holding hands with.

"No! They're mean!" the little girl responds.

"Not all of them. This one's nice; her name is Lolita," the woman says.

I miss those days when your biggest worry was whether the whale you were seeing was mean or not. At least she has her mom to hold her hand through it all.

We wait outside of the orca exhibit and my mom rummages through her purse. Finally, she pulls out the tickets to the 11:30 show, and we wait to get scanned in.

Pretty soon, we find ourselves sitting among the many, many people on the uncomfortable bleachers. As we sit down in the middle row to get a good view, I notice how small the tank looks. Surely, there's more space behind the scenes that we don't see? That concern quickly fades away as the show begins. It's a good thing I can't see my face right now because I know I look ridiculous. My face hurts from smiling this big of a smile. I can hear my heartbeat in my ears.

"This is Lolita, our killer whale!" one of the trainers calls out. Three trainers all aligned on a

For Tokitae

beam that separates the tank get ready for the performance.

Upbeat music starts blasting and I feel that excitement again as the stadium seats vibrate to the beat.

She jumps up, and a loud crash erupts, sending water splashing out in all directions. The crowd cheers and makes a chorus of *oooohs* and *awwws* as she jumps again.

The trainers give her a salmon, and then they start spinning. She mimics their movement. The crowd claps along to the beat of the song. Another salmon. Then, Lolita flips over so her white belly is facing the sky. A trainer climbs on and holds her flippers as they swim in circles along the edge of the tank. The crowd erupts in awe. I hear a child exclaim, "I wanna ride an orca!" Another salmon. She does a series of jumps and flips.

"Look at her!" my mom exclaims as she leans closer to me. I can't help but smile. She's so, so beautiful, and talented. I love her already. I turn and look at my mom, whose face is illuminated with wonder. I smile.

Chapter 10
Lolita

A few hours have passed by. The sun has moved quite a lot in the sky and is now shining almost directly down on my tank. People start to flood into the stadium, and I float up and kind of bob at the surface.

I scan their faces; they all look excited and thrilled to see my puppet show. I will admit it though, this is still probably the highlight of my day, even though it's still the same. Same tricks, same excited people, same cheers, same everything, blah, blah, blah… Still better than swimming in circles, though. I am happy to make everyone's day and I am glad that they are all here to see me; it makes me feel important.

By the time everyone is seated, we're all getting settled in for the show. I look over at the audience, lots of smiles. At least they're happy to see me. One human though, doesn't look too happy at first. Her eyebrows are drawn up. Her eyes dart to me, and then the rest of my tank. She still looks young, maybe the same age as Ellie. Maybe she's like Ellie and sees the show *my way*.

I don't know whether to feel relieved and grateful that she looks concerned, or guilty because she doesn't seem to be enjoying the show like everyone else. I think I feel a bit of both.

Her expression quickly changes as soon as the show starts, and she looks like she can't be contained, like she's so thrilled to be here that she wants to jump up or scream something. She looks at me again this time with her face more animated.

Pretty soon, I have to perform again.

Chapter Eleven
Cordelia

The show ends and we are all herded out. I take one final look at Lolita and take a deep breath in, trying to wrap my mind around it all and take it all in. I don't know if I'll ever see her again.

She floats lifelessly at the surface, facing my direction. She makes a sharp turn and swims back over to one of the trainers standing on the concrete barrier.

I watch as a girl walks around the corner and makes her way over to one of the trainers. She kneels getting closer to Lolita. Her eyes darting around her big black and white body. Her face is very familiar, but I don't know where I would know her from.

Lolita moves in quick and direct movements, swimming over and looking in my direction and back at the girl. The girl looks up, confused, but then that confused expression quickly fades into a surprised one. I watch her as she walks back over to her mom and asks her something that I can't hear. Then she walks around the wall and disappears.

My mom and I are still in the crowd heading out of her exhibit.

"What did you think?" Mom turns to me, her face bright with a smile flooding her cheeks.

"It was incredible. I loved seeing all her tricks." I smile.

"I know right? She was amazing!" she exclaims.

We finally push our way out of the crowd and stand in the main entrance for a second, before discussing where else to go. Somehow it feels like it's gotten even warmer over the past few hours. We head back out into the main part of the aquarium with people and families passing by. The air smells a little bit like the ocean but mainly like the fake food that they sell here. The smell of the ocean reminds me of Lime Kiln and I catch myself daydreaming about watching the

Southern Residents. The distant sound of people talking fills my head, and I'm pulled back into Miami, a completely different state on the other side of the country. And for the first time on the trip, I feel almost just a little bit homesick. If we do go to the beach on this trip, it's not even going to be the same ocean. Everything that feels like home for me is gone. Everything that I feel comfort in is gone: the evergreen forests, the calm, green ocean and the light, fresh air. Maybe that's why I liked the show so much, seeing her took me back home. If only for a moment, it still brought me back.

I look around, thinking about what we should do next, and surprisingly, I see the girl waiting around the corner. Once she sees me, she speed-walks up to me waving.

"Hi, do you remember me?" she asks. I scan her face, taken by surprise. I see that she is the girl I met at Lime Kiln who told me about Lolita in the first place.

"Yeah! From Lime Kiln? You were the one telling me about Lolita, right?" I ask in return.

"Yep. You were the one telling me about all

the Southern Residents?" she replies. I'm not sure if it's a question or a statement. She slowly breaks into a smile. It seems genuine and friendly.

"Yep," I try to mimic her smile but mine probably is much more of a nervous fake one. I always feel awkward talking to new people.

"That was my favorite part of that trip! It's funny that we meet each other again. I can't believe it! It's a small world I guess," she says with the slightest laugh. I can't believe it either; it's quite a coincidence.

"It really is. You guys know each other?" my mom chirps in with confusion in her voice.

"Yeah, we met at Lime Kiln while I was visiting Washington. What brings you two to Miami?" she asks.

"A trip," I say.

"Really? That's crazy! I see you on my trip, you see me on yours. I don't think I ever really introduced myself though. I'm Ellie," she says.

"Corey. It's nice to meet you," I laugh awkwardly. "Sorry, I don't know what to say since we already met." I laugh.

"Yep, you too. Have you ever been to Miami before?" Ellie asks laughing, too.

"Nope," I say.

"Maybe you need someone to show you around?" she offers.

This startles me. She barely knows me, and she's already trying to become friends with me. Maybe she's just trying to be polite though and felt pressured to talk to me because she recognized me? But then again, why would she offer to show me around if she was just trying to be polite?

My mom steps in, "Yeah, that'd be great, thank you."

"Thanks," I spit out.

"My brother and I aren't going to be at the aquarium tomorrow, are you guys busy? Or would you like us to show you around?" Ellie asks.

I look at my mom and wait for her response. "Yeah, tomorrow will be fine. We were going to pick up our rental car in the morning, but other than that, we were just going to explore."

"Great, well, can I text you where to meet? And is it alright if my brother tags along? He can drive and I can't so… yeah," she explains.

"Yeah, he can come, and you can text me," I reply. She hands me her phone and I put my number in.

"Cool. Well, I'll let you enjoy the rest of the aquarium and I'll see you tomorrow," Ellie says, waving goodbye.

Mom and I both thank her and then turn to leave. What just happened?

Chapter Twelve
Lolita

The crowd is filled with gleaming faces. I can feel the excitement radiating off of them. Not much happens here. Day after day I do the same shows, same pieces of training, same health checks, same blah, blah, blah…

I keep going though. You have to keep your head up or you'll drown… figuratively and literally. I still have my little freedoms, my little joys. I pay close attention to the little things and even though I've lost a lot, I don't take what I have for granted.

My heart feels happy whenever I look out to see those beaming faces. No matter how many times I see them, I love knowing that even if I can't be with my family, I can still mean something to people and their families.

I don't think all humans are bad. Ellie and her brother aren't bad. I don't think any of my trainers are, either. They all care about me deeply, but they're still caught in the web and are supporting the greedy people making money off of me while I'm stuck in this prison. I'm glad I'm not human, it sounds complicated. If I was human, I'd like to think that I'd be one of the good ones. One of the ones who bring hope to the world.

The crowd erupts into applause as the show comes to an end. The people move in a big blob of chaos and make their way to the gates. On the way out, I find a girl with her mom, stopped by the blob. The girl stares at me - she's the one who stood out to me in that crowd. Her earthy green eyes dart to my eyes and to my body floating at the surface. She reminds me a lot of Ellie, she looks like she's around the same age, and she still looks hopeful.

Looking directly in my eyes she smiles at me. Sometimes, if I'm lucky, Ellie will bring people back here to meet me. Maybe I could do some mischievous meddling and get them to be friends so I can meet her.

I turn and swim over to Ellie and turn back to this girl. Ellie looks up, sees her, and looks excited. She walks out.

I feel very mischievous.

Chapter Thirteen
Cordelia

The night faded into morning and dawn brought a reset on the city. The sky was a little cloudier than usual, but the air was still humid. The noise from all the night activity has died down quite a bit, but it's still a loud city.

We rented a small, silver Kia at about nine in the morning and headed back to our hotel room as we waited to hear back from Ellie.

"I've had so much fun," my mom says. Something about the tone of her voice sounds like that's going to change, like she's preparing to tell me bad news.

"Me, too," I agree.

"Well, yesterday was fun, but one of the reasons why we came here was because I was contacted about a job. Today's my interview. Would you be mad if I left you with Ellie and her brother? We'll spend the rest of the trip together, I promise," she compromises.

My mom works at a small art gallery in Friday Harbor, and she makes her art on the side. I'm not sure what job she got offered here, but I *knew* that there was going to be a catch to today. I should have known that there was more to this then just a mother-daughter bonding trip. That realization saddens me a little, but I try not to show it.

"It's fine," I say. "What's the job?"

"Drawing people's caricatures on a cruise ship," she replies.

"Oh…" my voice trails off. As much as I try to push it away, I am still disappointed. "Well, it's fine, I'll just get to know Ellie and her brother better."

"I'm sorry, sweetie. We'll spend tomorrow together," she says.

"Yep," I respond shortly.

Luckily, I feel my phone vibrate in the back pocket of my denim shorts. It's Ellie. My disappointment fades as I answer the phone.

We decided on a store to meet at

downtown and then we would just kind of walk around. When they said downtown Miami, I was picturing something like downtown Friday Harbor: streets lined with cute little shops and restaurants, music playing on the streets, very touristy. Downtown Miami isn't anything like that. Instead, it is busy; everywhere I look there are crowds and buildings. It is much more like Seattle, with towering buildings made of huge, shiny glass windows. The only plants I see are tall palm trees reaching out to the clear blue sky.

Pretty soon I see Ellie and her brother waiting for me on a bench on the sidewalk. I wave and walk up as my mom pulls away.

"Hi, Corey! This is my brother, Theo. Theo this is Corey," she introduces us.

"Hello," he greets me.

"Hi," I say, "Downtown Miami isn't anything like I expected," I say with a laugh. I look around and take it all in; it's very industrial and bright. It feels like when you pick up a book for the first time and don't know anything about it - new, mysterious in a way and that scares me. I worked myself up about it last night, worrying about saying something that might offend them. So today all I have to worry about is covering up my true dislike for their city.

"Yeah?" Ellie asks.

"Yeah..." I trail off.

"How so?" Theo asks.

"Well, when you were on your trip did you go to downtown Friday Harbor?" I answer with another question.

"Yup," they both say.

"I imagined it to be more like downtown Friday Harbor," I explain. "That's stupid though, isn't it?" I laugh. "I knew I was going to a city, and I still didn't expect this... *a city*."

"Well, we'll show you around. It'll grow on you, trust me," Ellie assures me.

We walk along the sidewalk for a while and dart into shops that are all too expensive to buy anything. It blew my mind. I thought that the downtown Friday Harbor shops could be unreasonably priced, but that wasn't anything compared to this.

We reach the artistic side of the city. It is filled with more art galleries and crazy architecture. The buildings reach up to the clear blue sky, some of the crazier ones twisting. People on the streets were conversing amongst themselves, or to themselves, sometimes it was hard to tell, and the roads were busy with traffic. It's hot out, but the breeze that comes off of the ocean cools us.

As we approach a park with more strange architecture and art, Ellie runs out in front of us, stretching her arms out, exclaiming enthusiastically, "Welcome to Miami!" A huge grin spreads across her face.

"Oh my god! Do you really have to always be this dramatic?" Theo exclaims in an exasperated tone as he rolls his eyes.

"Do you always have to ruin everyone's fun?" Ellie mimicked his tone.

"At least I don't act like I'm coming straight out of some freaking cartoon!" he returned.

"At least I don't -" Ellie started to say.

"Ellie, let's just keep going," Theo suggests. Yet it didn't stop there, the teasing went on and on. I continue to try to make small talk and just smile and not say anything too ridiculous while they're teasing each other.

Despite the awkwardness, I found it kind of fun to watch. Their play fighting was entertaining, they seemed so close. Close enough to completely slander each other, but with smiles on their faces. I wish I had a sibling, or at least a close friend.

"Corey, don't you agree?" Ellie asked.

I wasn't paying attention. "I'm sorry, agree with what?"

Theo interrupts and asks, "Doesn't Ellie remind you of some cringy Disney character?'"

"Oh, shut up," Ellie yells.

"I wasn't talking to you," he remarks.

Not wanting to take sides in this sibling war, I just smile and let there be a minute in silence.

"Well, what'd you think of the city so far?" she asks.

"It's beautiful, but different than I'm used to," I answer.

"Do you wanna keep going, or we could head down to the beach?" she asks.

"I'm not sure. You guys decide," I respond.

"Well, why don't we go down to the beach

and then head back here if we still want to?" Theo plans.

As we pull out, the glare of the window catches my eye, and I take one last look at the city as we drive off.

It didn't take long for us to arrive at the beach. It was different from the beaches back home. Instead of rocky, it was filled with almost white sand, and the water back home is calm, but here it was wavy like you see in the movies. I've never seen a beach with real waves. Although, what really stood out was the pounding music blasting from nearby beach bars. It's only eleven in the morning and I wonder how many of these people are drunk. The beach was so crowded with half-naked people that I could barely see the sand.

I don't know where to look without feeling like I am invading someone's privacy and scarring myself for life at the same time. I glance back at Ellie and Theo, who are both stifling laughter.

"What?" I say as I roll my eyes.

"Your face is amazing," Ellie says laughing

at me.

"Ellie, I think now would be a much better time to welcome her to Miami," Theo says laughing.

"I think you'd probably enjoy the beach more if we walked down a bit to get to the open part," Ellie says after they're finished laughing at my reactions.

"Please," I don't hesitate to reply.

After a very painful moment of swimming through the sea of people, we finally start to break through the crowed.

Once we get to the remote section of the beach, I finally relax and allow myself to enjoy the surreal tropical surroundings.

The ocean breeze brushes through my hair, and I take a deep breath of the salty air. I close my eyes, focusing on the wind and the smell of the ocean. It feels like home.

"Come on!" Ellie and Theo shout as they run towards the waves.

I run barefoot across the warm sand straight into the wind. It slaps against me, pulling me back. I feel like I could fly away in the wind if

I let it take me. I skip across the shallow water. I pause, stretching out my arms, realizing that the water is pulling back, very quickly and strongly. The next big wave comes. I run into it until it crashes down on us. It sweeps me off my feet and pulls me back into the sand. I'm amazed at how warm and clear the water is. Even on the hottest days back home, our water stays cold; refreshing, but cold. Here though, the water is warm and welcoming - not quite like bath water, but close.

"Woo-oh!" I shout. The bottoms of my shorts are soaked.

"You like the beach here?" Theo asks with a grin.

"Yeah," I laugh. "Not used to it though."

"You're not used to anything here it seems!" he teases.

Ellie runs over to us, water splashing up on her legs and shorts as she takes every step. She kicks the water splashing Theo but carefully avoiding me.

"What do you think?" she asks me with a giggle.

"It's fun, I like the waves," I say.

"These waves are nothing! They're barely even waves, trust me," she assures me.

"Okay?" I say.

She was right, the waves weren't much, they simply grazed the shoreline and kind of bobbed us up and down as we went deeper into the ocean. It was nice. I like it here.

We wade out pretty deep, and it takes us a while to head back. When we do, we decide to just walk across the shoreline for a little bit.

"So, Corey, what do you think of Miami and Florida so far?" Theo asks. His voice carries a very cheerful tone, and both he and Ellie seem to always have a smile.

"It's exciting, but also kind of terrifying since I've never traveled before," I say. I laugh and tilt my head, letting the sun spread across my face.

As we talk, we start making our way down the beach. Walking at first, but then we start to sprint, laughing, running down the beach, letting the sun shine down at us.

Theo isn't watching where he was going

and we see it before he does. "Stop!" Ellie and I yell. A section of the sand had been roped off. He stops in front of it, barely missing crashing right through the barrier.

"Come 'ere!" he shouts.

It was a green sea turtle nest. Stakes were sunken into the ground and a rope had been connecting them. A little sign read, "Green Sea Turtles Nesting Here." Thank God Theo didn't crash through that nest.

"Around this time of year, certain places on the beach are always roped off because of the nests. Pretty cool, huh?" Ellie explains.

"Yeah! Have you ever seen sea turtles?" I ask.

"Mhm, all the time. It always depends on the time of year though. Especially in mid to late May you get to see quite a few of them," she says.

"We can go to the bay and see manatees and maybe sea turtles still. It's early June so they'll probably still be there," he suggests.

"We should!" Ellie exclaimed. "I love manatees and sea turtles. They're the best!"

For Tokitae

"They're like her orcas," he laughs. Except I don't think they're like my orcas for her at all.

For Tokitae

Chapter Fourteen
Lolita

I hum a little tune over and over in my head. It's the same song that we've been playing during some of the shows today. I don't understand what most of the words mean but I can't get the beat out of my head.

It's gotten dark and almost everyone left. I'm alone, in the soundless dark of night. I'm not tired yet, physically. Mentally though… oh boy, I'm so exhausted! But, I have to keep in shape so I can do well in shows. So, I swim in laps around the tank, and each time I race myself going a little bit faster. The water crashes around me with every lap.

Okay, that was fun. Now what?

Without anything better to do, I float at the surface of the water for a few moments. The

For Tokitae

silence rings and cuts sharp into me, it's deadly. The nights are the worst of all because I'm so, so alone. But it's okay, I have the stars and the moon to keep me company.

So, I look up at the faint, but still twinkling stars for a while. It reminds me of my mom. Even though it was a long time ago, I still remember watching the stars with her. She'd tell me stories of how the sky was just like another ocean, and the stars were all little fish and the twinkling was their scales.

She used to sing me a song every night about those stars, and then I'd fall asleep with the rest of my family. I'd snuggle up close to her as we lay still at the surface of the water until it was time to start traveling again.

I wonder if she's looking at the same stars right now. I wonder if she still misses me.

I sing her song, as I so often do during the lonely nights. As I sing, I can hear her singing with me, her voice fitting perfectly in mine, harmonically, carrying on the sweet melody. She's far away, but her voice is still right here with me….Always present.

Chapter Fifteen
Cordelia

It's about a fifteen-minute drive to the bay that Theo told me about. I'm not even the one driving, and I don't like driving in the city. I guess I discovered that in Seattle though, too many cars, too much traffic.

When we finally get there, I step out of the car into the warm sun. I'm still wet from the first beach we went to, and the car was cold, so the sunshine feels nice. There aren't as many people or tall buildings here, but that makes sense, we're not in Miami anymore.

"So, how was your trip in Friday Harbor?" I ask them both.

"It was amazing! I love it there; it was so pretty, and I loved seeing the orcas," Ellie says.

"Yeah, and it was nice seeing family too," Theo says.

"Tell us more about the Southern Residents," Ellie requests.

"Like what?" I reply.

"Everything. How'd you get to know them? Why are they so special to you?" she asks.

"Story time," I joke. They both smile. The boards of the boardwalk bounce as we walk on them. I look to my left to see the clear blue ocean, and on my right, the siblings, and a line of palm trees.

"Well, I've never moved, so I've spent practically my whole life watching the whales. When I was little, my parents took me. In second grade, I became close to a friend whose grandparents work at the lighthouse. Back then my friend and her grandparents used to take me whale-watching. We used to sit for hours and Janice and Ed, her grandparents, would tell us everything about all the SRKWs. When I say everything, I mean *everything*... even about the individual orcas. I became really close to them and the orcas," I pause and smile to myself. "About a year after we became friends, she moved back with her parents in California. We haven't talked since. But I stayed friends with Janice and Ed, and nothing's changed with them, we still do all the same stuff like when I was little."

"I think they miss her a lot – their granddaughter, I mean. So, in other words, I kinda became like a granddaughter to them," I pause, then switch subjects quickly, "Really, I've kinda grown up with the orcas…? But I wasn't very aware that they were struggling until about four years ago." I pause again, remembering. "My parents had a really bad fight, so I asked Janice if she could take me to the beach for a little escape. When the Js came…" I trailed off and my memories took over.

I remember it so clearly. Both parents were furious, for a reason that I'll never understand.

Even hidden and contained in my little bedroom, the yelling echoed in my mind, making my blood run cold. Firsts are always the worst, because they always hit you like a brick wall and this was their first real fight.

I didn't know what to do. Fighting against the urge to just breakdown, I called Janice. Thankfully, she agreed to take me.

Time passed by so slowly. What was only a few minutes felt like an eternity before she arrived.

When we got to the lighthouse, we had to wait even longer for the Js to arrive. Even though I had calmed down a little bit, I was still upset, of course.

"Ohh…" Janice said as she looked at me concerned. "You're okay now."

"But what if something happens while I'm gone?" I sobbed. This thought weighed on my conscience.

"You did the right thing, you're okay now," her words as comforting and warm as a sunny day.

Too bad it didn't make a difference.

"It's okay," she kept telling me, "Here, we're going to try something. Close your eyes."

I closed them.

"Just listen. Tell me, what do you hear? Tell me everything you hear," she told me.

"I hear the ocean. I hear people talking. I heard you. I hear my breathing. I hear birds. I hear the wind," I told her.

"Now, tell me about today – what's the weather like?" she asked.

"It's windy, but the water is calm. The sun is out; it's a beautiful day," I said.

"Now focus on your breathing," she said.

I did. As strange as it may seem, she was teaching me how to calm down, and how to take in everything.

"Now what do you hear?" she asked. I couldn't see her, but I could hear her smile.

I listened. Everyone around me became quiet. I could hear the dorsal fin of an orca breaking the surface and the Pffft sound they made as they exhaled. It was a majestic sound. My heart started beating faster, my tears dried up and my smile came back.

"Orcas," I say.

"Open your eyes, girl!" she exclaimed.

All my problems faded into the ocean breeze... they didn't matter now. All that mattered were the orcas. They were so beautiful as they surfaced and exhaled. They looked as majestic as they sounded.

They were majestic because they're wild, that's what it was back then - the wildness and the freedom was the beauty of this creature. I didn't realize back then everything that I know about them now.

For Tokitae

There were so many of them, and they swam pretty close to the shore that day. I noticed Cookie J-38, he has a very tall dorsal fin, and an almost solid saddle patch, except one patch closest to his dorsal fin. His mother, Oreo J-22 was glued to his side, of course.

An orca jumped out of the water and breached, then crashed down again, looking so free.

But that's when we saw it. Tahlequah J-35, was carrying something on her back. I wasn't sure what it was at first. I turned to Janice, who had a tear running down her face. She looked horrified.

"What is it? What's she holding?"

She took a deep breath in, and her lip started to shake, but she managed to spit out, "A calf. She's carrying her dead calf."

A shiver went down my spine. I didn't know what to think. I looked back at Tahlequah, and surely enough it was a calf. There it was, the small baby laying still and lifeless.

Teary-eyed and with a heavy heart, I swallowed and watched as she struggled to hold her baby up to the surface. I remember how chaos spread through the park like a disease. Why would she be doing this? To try to get it to breathe? Maybe she's simply in grief.

Little did I know then that that was only day 1. It was only the start of her tour of grief.

"Tahlequah was carrying her dead calf on her back. It took everyone by surprise how long she carried her calf," I explained.

They both nod and wait for me to carry on.

So, I told them.

"Tahlequah carried her calf for *seventeen* more days and for over *one-thousand miles!* We hadn't expected it to go on that long, but she just couldn't let go. It was like she was in grief of this calf that she had just lost. She was unable to let go of the future it could've had, the memories she could've made with it. She loved her baby so much and wanted to hold on to that love. Finally, she let go… but, because I know the Southern Residents, I know that to this day, she still must love that baby she lost.

Over two weeks and three days of following her, she *finally* let go."

And that's when it clicked for me.

I realized I needed to accept the fact that

our family will never be perfect, and that I need to let go of that expectation.

"So, yeah, I guess that day was a big day for me. That was one thing that contributed to my little obsession of these orcas."

Both Theo and Ellie looked speechless. They stared awkwardly at me until Theo finally broke the silence.

"Wow," he says.

Ellie bounces over to me and puts her arm around me in a semi-hug. "That must have been an amazing experience." I could tell she didn't know what to say either.

The breeze blows over us, carrying me back home, as I still think about the orcas. A lot has happened in the last four years.

We walk along the boardwalk silently for a little way.

Finally, I break the silence, "Okay, I told you my orca story, now it's your turn. What's it like growing up with Lolita? Are you close to her? What's she like?"

"Well, story time," Ellie says with a smile.

And with that, we finally begin to approach the jetty.

For Tokitae

Chapter 16
Lolita

I think my favorite time of day is early morning, or – wait no, maybe it's night. Well, I guess I like both best for different reasons. I like night because I love seeing the stars, and singing in the silence.

When the sun first disappears, I'm in a pool of moonlight. I'll bob at the surface watching the shining of the sky-fish's scales. I can hear the ocean's waves off in the distance. At first it's peaceful, but then I get reminded of what I lost, and I feel so alone.

Some nights the fish don't come out and the moon is blurred away partially covered. Those nights are the worst, but I remember many, many nights like that at home, too. My family always said that we need to be thankful for the nights with many stars. If there are many fish in the sky, then they'll be many fish in the sea, right?

They would also say that the moon is what brings the fish. As the fish eat away at the moon, the stars grow stronger so they can make their way down to us. The moon grows back though, because the fish never take too much, they only take what they need so they don't run out. This is how my family teaches their young to live in balance with everything, because that's very important to us. It's something that the humans need to learn.

If we sing to the stars, it'll help them make their way to the sea. So, my mom and I would always sing together. I cherish those memories and honor her by still singing. Some nights I still hear my family's voices as they still sing along side me, even miles apart.

The morning is peaceful too though. The sun casts a warm glow and paints the sky in different colors as it pulls itself up, bringing the rest of us awake with it. Our sun never has anything eating away from it though. Instead of providing for the fish in the sky, it provides for us, lighting up the world and bringing warmth and comfort.

My mother is called Ocean Sun because she brings the sea warmth and comfort. Without her and the rest of my family, I rarely get that feeling anymore.

Although, I still love the mornings because everything feels new, fresh, as if the world had just reset. Before the people get here, I have time in the morning to take it all in and enjoy the sun coming up and the colorful sky. So many hours a day, and for so long, I always feel so gray, but the colors of the sky make me happy.

For Tokitae

Chapter 17
Cordelia

The sun casts a warm glow over the blanket of blue. We have climbed up the rocky jetty, and are looking out into the vast, calm ocean, watching the baby sea turtles take their first steps and head out into the water.

"Oh. My. God. They are so cute! I just want to scoop one up and put 'em in my pocket!" Ellie leans forward to get a better look at the turtles.

I can't help but laugh. They *are* pretty adorable. They wobble out across the white sand leaving little dents in it. Theo glances at me from the corner of his eye, grinning to himself. He leans in closer to me and whisperers, "She's seen sea turtles a thousand times, you'd think it was her first."

I laugh breathily, looking over at her then

For Tokitae

back to him, and I whisper back, "Well, I meannn, look at them."

"Oh no, not you, too!" he jokes as he shakes his head and squints at me in disgust.

A smile turns up the corners of my mouth. "Hey! I get an excuse; this *is* my first time seeing them!"

He raises his eyebrows, letting out a long sigh, but then quickly smiles. "I guess that's true."

A moment passes without a word being said as we watch and adore the little turtles. Once they crawl across the sand and make it to the water, you can see them start to glide in it, and then fly away. I have always had a deep love and fascination for aquatic animals. Maybe it's because the ocean seems like it's an entirely different world than our own.

"Hey, you know what I just realized?" Theo asks, still in a hushed voice.

"What?" I reply, in a tone that mimics his own.

"We never answered your question," he says with a smile.

"Nope, you didn't bother," I reply as I roll my eyes.

"You ever gonna answer, Corey? Huh?" he nudges her.

"Oh! Yeah! I got distracted, sorry," she says. She glances back at the turtles, then looks into my eyes. "Well, to be honest, I hate the city. I hate all the people and would much rather be somewhere more natural. But, I absolutely love the beaches and the weather and everything about Florida, except Miami. We lived outside of the city in a little house, until I was about nine. My mom was a stay-at home mom, and my dad would drive into the city and work there. I loved our old house. We were on the beach, and I used to be able to go snorkeling and swimming." She pauses and frowns. "Then my dad got sick. He couldn't work, so we had to move to the city so my mom could work instead. He's gotten much better, which is amazing, but he still hasn't fully recovered."

Although it's a been a limited number of days that I've known her, when she talks about her dad, that bright shine in her that I *do* know seems to disappear. Naturally and without missing a beat, Theo picks it up as he tries to brighten her mood.

"Dad's getting better though. Think about it, Ellie, if we hadn't moved out here, we wouldn't have met Lolita. Why don't you tell her about that?" he nods.

"Oh, well she's amazing. She has just the sweetest personality, and she's so loving. She always gets super excited to see us. I've known her since I was nine, and a lot has happened over those last six years, but she's been there for me through it all." Her eyes glisten like the ocean, but her smile tries to creep back onto her face as she talks about Lolita.

"So, she's really impacted your life, huh?" I ask.

They both nod.

"It's amazing how animals can do that," I say.

The sky changes to shades of pink and orange, and the sun slowly starts to disappear beyond the horizon, just like those little turtles. We turn around and start to head back home again. All of us with smiles on our faces, and a peaceful feeling in our hearts.

Before I know it, I'm saying goodbye to Ellie and Theo Holloway as the sky starts to darken and the night life starts bustling. I hope I get to see them again.

"Corey, when are you going home?" she leans against her car, with her legs out and crossed, still covered with sand and ocean water.

"In two days," I reply.

"Well, try to stop by the aquarium again, we'll see about introducing you to Lolita." They smile at me and climb into their car.

I wave as they drive off.

The scene around me changes into the comfort of our little hotel room, my mom sprawled out across the bed, tuned into the tv.

"Hey, honey," she calls as I walk in.

"Hi. How'd the interview go?" I ask.

"It went really well. I think they liked me," she says.

"I'm sure they did," I say in a short tone.

For Tokitae

"I'm so sorry about leaving you again. Did you have fun with your new friends?" she asks.

"Yes, actually. They were both super nice. We got along well, and they invited me to meet Lolita tomorrow! I'm so excited!" all the nervousness from earlier that day seems to settle, and now all that I can think about is meeting Lolita.

"Honey, that's great!" she says. "So, you'll be on your own for a little tomorrow, too?"

I resist the urge to roll my eyes because she's calling me *honey,* one more time, when I know she's just trying to sweet talk me.

"I mean….Yeah?" I say bitterly.

"I'm sorry. We'll do something together later tomorrow and the next day before we have to go home," she reassures me.

The next day, my mom drops me off at the aquarium and leaves to go explore the city a little bit on her own. I bet I look really ridiculous again, with another goofy grin. I walk with my chin up barely even stopping to look at any of the other marine life and I make a bee-line to her exhibit. On my way, I call Ellie to let her know I'm coming. By the time I get there, I'm pretty much out of breath. My heart starts to race as I meet Ellie outside of her exhibit.

"Hiya!" she calls out to me. She waves excitedly reaching up and quickly waving her hand with her outstretched fingertips. "You came just in time! She has an entire half-hour between shows, so we should be good for a while to hang out."

"I'm literally shaking! I'm so excited," I say. I know now that I look ridiculous too, like a little kid on Christmas morning.

We head behind this fence that says, "employees only" and turn around to the back side of the tank.

"'Employees only,' I feel like such a rebel!" I joke.

"Yep. Look at you, breaking all the rules," she teases back.

We step out onto the barrier of her tank. At this point I can hear my heartbeat echoing throughout me, and I feel alive.

And there she is, floating in the water only a few feet from me.

For Tokitae

Chapter 18
Lolita

The morning fades away as the sun dances across the endless blue expanse. I've already done a bit of training today, one show, and now I am just resting and trying to enjoy the day as much as I can anymore.

Yesterday I didn't get to see Ellie or her brother Theo. I get to see them on most days though - usually not more than one or two days in a row goes by with their absence. I like being with *some* people, especially them.

The sun shines almost directly above my little tank and I drift upon the gentle waves. It shines down on my back and I let it define me, but only for a moment. The sound of footsteps arises from around the corner, I see two figures moving like shadows slipping from one place to another as they make their way into the light.

It's Ellie with the girl who I noticed during the show.

Ellie greets me enthusiastically and introduces me to her friend, Corey. I fly through the water and poke my head up to where they can see me and touch me if they want to. Her expression is tense and sharp. She relaxes, and the smile gleams across her face into a ridiculous grin. Ellie whispers something to her, making me frustrated that I can't hear.

She opens her mouth to speak to me, and what she's saying makes my heart stop entirely. Her eyes bare into mine, and she talks about my family. *My family.*

It's been so long since I last heard someone talk about my family. She tells me how important they are to her and how she knows that they still miss me.

And there I go. I'm gone. Swept away with relief but still yearning for them. If I were human, I know that I would have the exact same expressions as she: so, *so*, happy. She *knows* my family; she *knows* they miss me!

I don't know that I've ever met a person like Corey. Maybe there is still hope that I'll get to see them again.

For Tokitae

Chapter 19
Cordelia

It's a dreamlike feeling that I am immersed in entirely. It's surreal, being here, seeing her, being up close to her. Yet it is exciting. So, so exciting. Lolita is so beautiful, almost otherworldly.

"Hi, Lolita! I brought you a friend!" Ellie calls out to her.

She glides through the water and pokes her head above the surface about an arms-length away from me. I kneel next to her on the work island Ellie and I sit on. I can hear every heartbeat like a drum, echoing throughout my body, making me shaky, but in a good way. All the emotions that have been building up to this moment flood out of me and that brick that's been weighing me down gets lifted. Being here with her gives me this indescribable feeling that I can only compare to the one that overcomes me when I'm watching the Southern Residents back home. I feel at home.

Ellie smiles at me, leans closer, and says in a hushed voice, "Talk to her, it'll make her happy."

"Okay," I breath in slowly, and smile at her. "Hi, Lolita. I'm Corey. I know your family very well."

Lolita looks me dead in the eye, and she smiles back. I know she can't understand me. I think she can't, right? Part of me feels ridiculous talking to her. Yet, some part of me feels like she must. I decide I need to keep talking to her.

"They've taught me so much," I tell her.

She swims in a little closer and puts her head on the barrier that Ellie and I sit on.

"She wants to be pet," Ellie says.

"Really? Can I do that?" I ask.

"Yep. Here." She grabs my hand and gently guides it across the top of Lolita's head. "Think of her like a big, wet, hairless dog," she laughs.

I laugh too. "I can see why she's so special to you."

"She's already special to you, isn't she?" Ellie asks.

I nod.

"Isn't it funny how animals can do that?" she asks while the smile spreads across her face.

I brush my hand across her wet skin in a back-and-forth motion while looking into her eyes. "You're a special orca, aren't you?"

She smiles back at me. I wish she could talk back to me, but that question is unnecessary, for I already know the answer.

I rest my hand on her head, and I sit there with her. It's just me, Lolita, and Ellie. We sit in silence for a moment, and I think about how lucky I am.

"Hey! You must be Corey?" A trainer walks around the corner and approaches me. She looks just like Ellie, with the same friendly smile on her face.

"Yeah, hi! You must be Ellie and Theo's mom?" I ask.

She nods, "Would you like to give her a salmon?" she asks.

"Absolutely!" I beam.

She pulls out a white five-gallon bucket that reeks with the smell of fish.

"Show her what you have and then she'll open her mouth and just carefully slide it in, 'kay?" she explains as she tosses me a fish.

"'kay," I hold up the salmon. Its scales are slimy and the smell makes me gag, but I'm still more than grateful to give it to her. Surely enough, Lolita opens up her mouth telling me she's ready for it. I slide it to her, and she gulps it down and smiles back at me.

"Have you seen her shows?" she asks.

"Yeah, it was great," I reply.

"Well, if we had more time, I'd show you some of the training procedures. But I'm afraid we're going to have to say good-bye for now. Keep in touch and we'll see about bringing you back here again to help with training if you'd like?" she says as she puts away the bucket.

"Yeah, that'd be great! Thank you!"

I reluctantly stand up looking at Lolita from the gate one last time. She floats at the surface of her tank, holding her head up, her body cutting through the bright unnatural blue surface of the tank. Her tank isn't that big - compared to her - at all. She makes up a large proportion of it, and she doesn't seem to do too much in that tank other than swim laps or float.

A sudden peg of sharp guilt and a deep sadness for Lolita hits me.

"Ellie?" I get her attention.

"Hm?" she says.

"Is that the only tank that she stays in?" I ask.

"Yeah, why?" she answers.

"It's rather small, isn't it?" I say.

"I dunno, she has room to swim, so…" she shrugs. "I really gotta go now, talk later?"

I nod. "Thank you so much!"

"Of course," she says as she walks away.

All the way back to the hotel I couldn't stop thinking about Lolita. I have this strange feeling in my gut that I can't quite put words to. As soon as we get back to our hotel room I flop onto my bed, pull out my phone, and search "who's Lolita the orca?" then I scroll through the articles before settling on one called, "Save Lolita."

At the top of the page, is a small paragraph that says:

A four year-old killer whale named Tokitae was brutally taken from her mother in the Puget Sound and brought to the Miami Seaquarium where she was placed in a 35 foot wide tank and renamed 'Lolita.' She has lived there ever since.

Tokitae? So, Lolita must be like her stage name. I scroll down a ways to find the headline, "Her Story." My eyes dart through the text that reads:

On August 8, 1970, in the waters of the Puget Sound of Washington State, a pod of killer whales was attacked and rounded up by a group of killer whale herders led by Ted Griffiths and Don Goldsberry. Using speedboats, and an airplane, and releasing explosives into the water, they forced the orcas into Penn Cove. The juvenile orcas were separated from their mothers, as the infants were prime candidates to be sold to aquariums, while the adult orcas were released and free to leave. However, the adult pod would not leave their offspring and refused to swim free, vocalizing human-like cries until the last baby was pulled out of the water, never to return. One adult and four infant orcas were killed during this capture. In an attempt to keep the orca deaths from the public, the industry instructed the herders to slit open the bellies of the dead animals, fill them with rocks, and sink the creatures with anchors, hoping they would never be discovered. Because of the large number of violent orcas captured by the marine park industry in Washington State waters, an entire generation of orcas was eliminated. As a result, this orca population is now considered an endangered species. (Save Lolita- Raising Awareness for Lolita the Orca.)

    I pause and stare at the block of text, unable to comprehend it completely. Then it gets through to me; I realize what it's saying. My head hurts and heat rushes to fill every inch of me. *Why? Why would they do this? What the hell?*

    Here I am, sitting alone in a hotel room, fists clenched bitterly staring at the bright but little screen of my phone. The phrases *"Using speedboats and an airplane,"* and *"releasing explosives into the water, they forced the orcas into Penn Cove,"* keep replaying in my mind. Just thinking about that makes me want to throw up. I cannot even begin to imagine what it'd be like, to be an orca, who relies on communication, to have to go through this. To this day, the Southern Residents suffer from boat vessel noise. All that noise alone must have been horrible for them.

"The juvenile orcas were separated from their mothers." That phrase. That phrase sticks with me, echoing in my mind. I think back to my parents first *real* fight, the day that Tahlequah carried her dead calf. The Southern Residents rely so much on their families, the children never leave their moms. They just don't. I can't imagine how traumatizing it would be to be separated in that situation.

I feel sick to my stomach. I've only read two paragraphs, and I've had enough. I turn off my phone and chuck it to the end of the bed. I turn over, scoop up my pillow, and hug it tightly against me.

I can't stop thinking about it. That's horrible. Poor Tokitae. She was deprived of everything that it means to be a Southern Resident orca. Being able to hunt, and play, and share food, and communicate with her family. She was deprived of the freedom of being able to swim for hundreds of miles. She was deprived of her family. And they even changed her beautiful name!

I hate this feeling of restlessness and not being able to sit still. I need to do something, but I don't want to do anything. Out of lack of anything better to do, I pick up my phone and call Janice and Ed. Maybe they'll know something about it.

"Hello?" Janice answers.

"Hey, um, do you know who Tokitae is?" I ask. Part of me hopes that she'll say no, then I won't have to be mad at her for not educating me about this sooner. On the other hand, I need to know more.

"Yes. Haven't I told you about her?" she asks.

"No, I don't think so," I say. I know she hasn't because I haven't heard her full story until now.

For Tokitae

"Well, I should've. It's just a sad story to tell. I guess part of me never wanted to," she pauses, "I'll tell you about this, if you tell me all about your trip!"

I really don't have the patience right now to just talk about that, but I should've expected this from Janice. "Okay," I start, just trying to get the small talk over with. "Well, I thought mom has actually tried to redeem herself, so for a while I was trying to give her a chance, but, I found out the only reason she wanted to take me on this trip was because she got this fancy job offer. So, that sucks. But I became friends with these kids whose mom works at the aquarium where Tokitae lives, and I learned so much about her and even got to meet her and I made friends really quickly!"

"Oh, honey that's great! I mean, I'm sorry about your mom, but that doesn't come as a surprise to me," she scoffs. "So, I suppose you want to hear more about Tokitae after meeting her, huh?"

"Mhm,"

"Well, she was born in the L pod,

supposedly Ocean Sun's her mom; but you know, we never really know. In 1970 there was a huge orca capture. Lots were killed and that has changed the Southern Residents because they lost an *entire* generation! Ocean Sun still searches for her, of course, and none of the Southern Residents have returned to Penn Cove since that day," she explains.

"I can't believe that! That's horrible!"

"It gets worse. She was the only survivor of the orcas who got captured, and she was sold to the Miami Seaquarium, where she has been on display ever since then. Her tank is the *world's smallest* orca tank. I mean, you saw it. It's too small for her! She can't even dive! It's horrible! She's stuck swimming in circles and floating at the surface! And she still cries home for her family! Oh Corey, I hate this. It's not right," her voice starts to break.

"I know… I know. I don't know what to even say," I cry. I remember talking to her, I remember the look in her innocent face. People have put her through too much.

I've felt sad before, but even that was

different. I'm not scared. But there's this empty feeling in me that seems to linger, yet at the same time there's this anger that is boiling over me. As I look out my window into the street, I know that she doesn't belong here in Miami. Yet I just sit here. Confined to this hotel room with cold feet, and a sunken feeling.

Janice continues listing off what seems to be the countless injustices that this whale faces every day.

"She's being fed rotten fish, the water isn't clean, she's cramped in there, and we all know that she misses her family very, very much. All this so greedy humans can make money! It's awful!" she exclaims.

"It is!" I agree, "is there anything being done about it?"

"Yes. There are several different organizations who are trying to partner with the Seaquarium to get her freed. They have an entire plan and they're waiting to set it to action. But, honey, I fear that the owners of the aquarium aren't going to let her free until she's too withered for them to make any money off of her.

At that point, she won't be healthy enough to return home." Her doubtful words repeat in my thoughts.

"Well, we just can't let that happen. What can we do?" I ask.

"I don't know. There are probably lots of people you can talk to, lots of organizations to support. It's too big and too sad of a problem for me. I wish I could do something, too," she says, her voice empty.

"I'll figure something out. Thanks, Janice. I'll see ya' in a few days!" I say as I hang up.

Quickly, without giving anything a second thought, I pull up that website again, https://www.savelolita.org/ and I read so fast that I barely give my mind time to understand anything.

As I scan through the article, some key things stand out most to me. For example:

Lolita currently lives alone with no other killer whale companions. When not performing in her show, Lolita floats listlessly in her tank. In the wild, killer whales swim hundreds of miles daily, diving as deep as 500 feet. In her tank, she swims in circles inside the 35-foot-wide area and can only go as deep as 20 feet in a small area in the center of the tank.

Lolita is the oldest living killer whale in captivity, in the smallest orca tank in the country.

There are no words that began to justify how tragic her story really is. She has to be the loneliest orca in the world. I scroll back up to the top of the page, and I watch the little video. It talks about how we can't let her die alone.

That phrase sticks with me.

Don't let her die alone…

I'm going to try to help her, *I won't let her die alone.*

Chapter 20
Tokitae

As she heads out, she leaves that grateful feeling with her. Even though our time together was limited, I feel as if Corey and I have some sort of connection. This cannot be true. Can it? It seems like centuries ago that someone has spoken of those who used to be so close to me.

    I swim laps racing myself every single time, creating waves that splash up against my face and body as I surface and dive, and surface and dive, faster, faster, faster! I fling myself out into the air, and feel the breeze against my wet skin. Mid-air I let out a cry of excitement, and I crash back down against the pool of unnaturally blue water.

    It may not be a big deal to you. You might think that I'm easily amused and am being dramatic about something that is only microscopic in the bigger picture. And I'll give you that, I *am* easily amused, but it's because I must be. I have to be happy and grateful for the little things or else what's the point? We should all be more grateful, I think.

Yet, she's not the only human who's made me feel this way. Throughout my captive life, there have been many people who have made my day repeatedly. There are lots of kind people who have made me happy and grateful, and hopeful. Like my trainers, and quite a lot of the people who come to visit me, there are a lot of people who mean something to me.

In the grand scheme of things, I know that maybe I am just a marionette. I must be used to the never-ending puppeteer pulling at my strings, stuck in the constant oppression, as the deceitful continue to get their pockets filled.

Although, I will say, knowing that I *do* make a difference in people's lives, is special and I know I have to hold onto that, because not all humans are puppeteers, and I know that quite a few of them are marionettes just like me.

Chapter 21
Cordelia

As soon as I'm able to wrap my mind around everything, and completely understand Tokitae's story, I call Ellie and Theo. I listen to the loud beeping sound my phone makes as I dial in her number. Although now I'm starting to second-guess myself. They're both so close to her, what if they don't want to hear this? It'd be hard because I'm sure they'd want whatever is best for Tokitae, but they probably wouldn't want to let her go.

Despite my conflicted thoughts, I figure that Ellie would want to hear this, that she deserves to hear this. I press call.

"Hello?" she answers.

"Hey," I say.

"Oh! Corey! How are you?" she asks, happy

For Tokitae

to hear from me.

"I'm fine. What about you?" I respond.

"I'm good. Just got home from school and I'm heading to the Seaquarium to see mom and Lolita. Theo's driving, should I put you on speaker phone or...?" she says.

"Sure, I don't care."

"So, do you know who Tokitae is?" I ask, already knowing my answer.

"No... why do you sound sad? Are you alright?" she asks.

"Fine. I just want to tell you something. I'm gonna send you an article. Don't be mad, I know how much she means to you, but you should know about this," I tell her. I hang up and send her the article called "Save Lolita." I cross my fingers that she won't get too upset.

While I wait for Ellie to call me back, I keep replaying what I learned in my head. What I got from the article was, pretty much, Tokitae was captured from the L pod in 1970, it was a *horrible, brutal* capture, and because of it we lost an entire generation of orcas. The only juvenile who was captured that survived was named

Tokitae. Tokitae was sold to the Miami Seaquarium where her name was changed to Lolita. At first, Lolita had a companion, Hugo. Hugo was an orca just like her. They got along really well, until he probably got too tired of living in a 35-foot-wide tank and he swam head-first into the tank wall over and over until it killed him. Tokitae/Lolita hasn't seen another orca since. Which kills me because I know how much the Southern Residents rely on each other, and she hasn't seen another orca since then.

By Animal and Plant Health Inspection Service (APHIS), her tank is illegal. It violates all the standards for size requirement. On the website, https://www.savelolita.org/, it states,

Lolita is approximately 21 feet long and 7,000 pounds. Per the guidelines, the tank for a killer whale the size of Lolita must be at least 48 feet wide in either direction with a straight line of travel across the middle. Lolita's tank is only 35 feet wide from the front wall to the slide-out (work island) barrier*. It is 20 feet deep at the deepest point and a mere 12 feet deep around the edges. The Miami Seaquarium needs significant repairs, and per the Marine

For Tokitae

Mammal Inventory Report, it has a substantial death rate for its animals.

Think about it: it says that Tokitae is 21 feet long, and the deepest section of her pool is only 20 feet deep. She wouldn't even be able to dive! The conditions of her tank are unjust and horrible! She is being deprived completely of the life that she deserves!

Organizations have come up with a plan to bring her back home, thankfully! They plan to build a sea-pen in a cove in San Jaun Islands for her to live. By doing this, they won't be throwing her back in the middle of the ocean after living the majority of her life under constant care.

There's this weight in my stomach knowing that I saw her, I was face-to-face with her, and I didn't see the pain in her eyes the way I see it now. I know now that I need to do something... and Ellie and Theo *need* to call me back. I really hope that they're not mad at me for showing them or suggesting those things.

I tap my foot onto the floor as I pull out my little rock from Lime Kiln and brush my thumb over it repeatedly, I stare at the ground and wait.

Ring

R-

"Hi," I say, answering it just as fast as I can.

"Hey… I um, I read the article," she says. Her voice sounds empty, cold, without even seeing her I know that her spark of constant excitement is gone. "Is it," she pauses, "-is it true?"

I pause, letting the silence take over us, then I sigh, "Yeah. I wish it wasn't though."

I hear her sigh over the phone. "Will I be able to see you again?"

"Maybe. I'll ask my mom and find out the schedule," I say.

"Well, we need to do something about this. I mean, I'm not sure what. I just need to see you so we can talk about it. I showed Theo too. Of course it made us both upset because we *do* care so much about her. I absolutely hate that this is happening. And I *hate* that I didn't know," she says with a sound like she's holding back a sob.

"Yeah. I know." I search my brain but I'm at a loss for words.

"I mean, now that I think about it, her tank

is tiny. She *does* float around or swim in circles. Her life is too routine," she says.

"I hate it," I say.

"Me too. I don't know why I hadn't questioned it until now either." Her tone that was once slow and empty fills with rage and I can't tell if she's crying or not.

"I'm sorry for telling you. Now I feel horrible," I sigh.

"No! Please don't feel bad. Thank you for sending me this. I somewhat knew because people have been protesting here all my life. I didn't think much of it because my mom always dismissed it as we're taking care of her, she doesn't have to starve, we can give her health checks. But now I realize that's only a small thing in the bigger picture. I think before, I just didn't care enough because I needed her too much, so thank you for showing me." she explains.

"Okay," I say.

"And I'm going to see her right now and so that'll help. I gotta go though. But I'll talk to you later?"

"Yeah, I'll text you to let you know when I

can see you again," I say.

"Okay, see you later." She hangs up.

The last full day of our trip has come, and mom wants to spend it together. It's weird, the past several days have gone by like they were caught in the wind, meanwhile I'm just floating along with it.

Because I got to choose to go to the aquarium, I let mom choose where we're going today. So, she decides to take me to a street art gallery.

I step out of the rental car and take a deep breath of the warm air. As we start to walk closer, I see the colorful artwork that decorates the walls. The bright colors stand out from the rest, and I get lost in the surreal paintings. Mom pulls me out of my little fantasy when she asks, "I don't think I ever got the chance to ask you about Lolita yesterday."

"Tokitae, mom, that's her real name," I correct her.

"What?" she asks. Her eyebrows pull

together, and her face looks very confused.

I explain to her the brutal capture, and the horrid conditions of the deprived life that she is living now. Then I switch to telling her about the bright side of things, about the plan to bring her home.

"My new friends and I want to help her, but we're not quite sure how," I tell her.

"Well, doesn't your friend's mom work at the aquarium?" she asks.

I nod.

"Maybe you could ask her if there's any way you guys could talk to the people in charge there," my mom suggests.

"Yeah! Too bad we only have today before we get home," I say. Now that I'm starting to get used to Miami, I'm beginning to dread leaving.

"What about the people who are already trying to bring her home?" she asks.

I gasp as I realize that there are people around where *I* live that I can get on board with.

Chapter 22
Tokitae

I immerse myself into the pool of black ink dotted with the lights of the beautiful sky fish's scales. I tilt my head up letting the pale moonlight enhance it, listening to the quiet night. I listen closely only to hear my mother's voice singing the songs that will never be forgotten.

    Tonight feels different, but in a good way. In many nights of the past, I was left with nobody but my thoughts, and the loneliness was tedious, it cut to the bone. In the silence I would wallow and mope about all I had lost, forgetting to be grateful for what I still have.

    I do still have a lot. I am very privileged in many ways. I now get to bring meaning to the lives of others; they can see me perform and it brings smiles to their faces. Those smiles and the night songs are all I had to live for before, it feels different now.

    Now I know that there is still hope in the world. I saw it in Corey and I see it in Ellie and Theo. Corey spoke of my family, I now know that they *are* alright, and they must miss me as much as I miss them. I still feel them every single day. Feeling their presence, their love, is something I never lost. Now I might have the chance to be reunited with them at last. Now, not only do I live for the smiles and the night songs, but I also still live for hope.

For Tokitae

Chapter 23
Cordelia

The next morning was rushed. I stuff one of those stale raisin hotel breakfast muffins in my mouth and grab my suitcase as we head out the door. Thankfully for me, my mom was understanding and is letting me head back to the Miami Seaquarium one final time to say goodbye to Tokitae and the Holloway siblings.

It feels weird driving through the city today knowing that this will be my last day to take it all in. Mom taps her hand eagerly as we drive, and she mumbles things anxiously to herself. I look up at her GPS only to see that we are about to be stuck in traffic… *of course*. And as we were warned, soon the car comes to a stop.

I sigh. I feel the warm glass under my forehead as I lean on the window looking out, trying to memorize the city one last time.

"I can't believe it's the last day," I say softly.

"I know," her words linger in the air, not matching her voice.

"Whatcha thinking about?" I ask as I sit back up.

"What you were telling me about that orca." Her words float about in the air along with the silence. Finally she speaks again, "Look, I know I haven't been the best mom, but just thinking about what it'd be like to have to watch my child be taken from me, without knowing where she is for so long and not being able to do anything about it, it kills me to even think about that."

"I know. That's why we have to do something for her then," I say, trying to brighten the mood.

Is it possible to feel sad and happy at the same time? Right now, I feel sad that this will be the last time I see her, and I feel sad knowing all that I do about her past. Yet, I feel happy knowing I'm making my way to see Tokitae and my friends, and that we're going to help her. This can't be my last time seeing her, it doesn't feel real. Yet it is.

I find Ellie and Theo in the crowd, and I start walking faster and speed up to them, leaving my mom in the dust.

"Hi!" I shout.

"Hey!" says Ellie.

"I'm glad you got to come one more time before you have to leave," Theo tells me.

"Yeah, me too!" I smile at them.

My mom finally catches up and I realize she has only met Ellie.

"This is my mom," I introduce her to my friends.

"Nice to meet you Ms...um?" he says politely.

"Hart," I tell him.

"Nice to meet you Ms. Hart," they both say.

She laughs, "Just call me Jenna."

"I'm Theo and this is my sister, Ellie, who I believe you already met."

"Are, are you ready to meet Tokitae?" Ellie asks excitedly.

"Yes," mom says. I can hear the apprehension and compassion in her voice.

I take deep breaths in as we walk into her encounter. As we approach her, it becomes more real to me. I see her tank, I see the way she floats lifelessly, I see the pain in her eyes. She swims over to me, and I try to blink back the tears.

I can't though... I break and I become a mess. But she just sits there, looking at me, her head an arms-length away from me. I look back at her, and we just kind of stare at each other for a moment.

"I think she'd be okay with it if you pet her," Ellie says. I realize that she and her brother are both trying to blink back tears, too. I turn to my mom, who's sitting right beside me, and realize she's even more of a mess than I am, and she hasn't even gotten to know Tokitae like I have.

I take her hand, squeeze it, and guide it over to Tokitae, and we both stroke her head. Her skin is soft and slick, feels almost rubbery.

I stare at her again, thinking about how

much she really has impacted our lives within such a short time. It's funny how animals can do that, isn't it? I keep saying it, but it's true. As I look back at her, I can see it in her eyes, *Tokitae knows*.

I turn and look at them both. "How did you not know?"

"We knew that people had a problem with it. But honestly, I didn't think she could return back to the wild. I didn't think any animals could," Theo explains.

"I dunno. I thought she was happy. But now it's clear that she isn't," Ellie adds as she wipes away the tears from her eyes.

It's funny how sometimes we only see things we *want* to see, and we only believe things we *want* to believe, despite the truth.

"We're gonna do something right?" I solemnly ask.

Ellie smirks, "Well a little mischievous scheming won't hurt anyone."

I smile.

"Corey, we gotta go. I'm sorry," mom says.

"But we've only been here for a few

minutes!" I say as my voice breaks. The tears come faster now.

"I know, but we have to say good-bye," she says.

Good-bye. Good-bye. Good-bye. That word repeats in my head. I don't want to say *good-bye*. I can't say it. A fire spreads inside my head. I will go back home and everything will go back to normal. Yet, Tokitae will be left here. It isn't fair!

"Do you want to hug her? Would that help?" Ellie asks.

"Can I?" I ask.

"Yes, let me show you," she says. She leans closer to Tokitae and starts to pet the top of her head. Then she leans in and wraps her arms around her. And Tokitae leans into the embrace too.

After pulling apart from Ellie, I move closer to her. Tokitae swims closer to me, and I pet the top of her head, lean closer and wrap my arms around her. She gently leans closer into me, putting her trust in me. I feel warm and loved by this animal that I only met a few days ago. I don't want to leave her. It makes me mad knowing what she's been through, I want to change things for her. I can't leave her *here*. She's not free anymore. I wish I could take her home with me, but I know I can't.

"I promise to try to help you," I whisper to her. My tears run down my face and fall on the top of her head. "And I'm sorry for everything."

I don't want to let go. I close my eyes and try to memorize this moment - the warmth and the love and care and sadness and regret and dread. And I whisper, "Good-bye, Tokitae."

Ellie and Theo walk us out, and I feel sad leaving them, too – not as sad as leaving Tokitae though. For the first time in a long time, I have real friends, and I won't even get to know them better. I don't want to say more good-byes. I think I've cried out all my tears, but I might have more for them.

For the first time since we've been here, I feel a little cold with the breeze. I close my eyes and imagine the breeze carrying all my sadness away. It helps a little, until I remember again.

They both hug me.

"Thank you for being friends with the

stalker girl you found at the aquarium," Ellie says with a laugh.

"Thanks for being friends with the 'dorca' you met at the lighthouse," I reply with a sad smile.

We all laugh and then I get in the front seat of our car and drive away. I stare out the window taking in the city for the last time.

Before I know it, I'm sitting in the window seat of the plane, and I hear the voice overhead telling me to buckle my seatbelt.

I prepare for takeoff, and as we get into the air I stare back out into the city as it gets smaller and smaller. I whisper, "Good-bye."

Chapter 24
Tokitae

The crowd is all bunched together trying to make their way through the gates, excitedly talking and smiling, and I am left to watch as they disappear. I know that many of them I'll never see again. It's a strange feeling, day-by-day for years and years, thousands of people watch me perform. The vast majority of them will never come back. The people who do return, I often recognize though. Even if they look different years later, I recognize them. I'm very proud of my attention to detail, not going to lie.

    I swim in small circles for the simple reason of passing time before something interesting happens to me again. I'm mid-circle when, out of the corner of my eye, I see four people walking up towards me. Corey, Ellie, Theo, and another woman who looks much older than all of them, make their way to the work island.

The woman who I didn't recognize has the same face shape as Corey, but quite a few different features.

That's a hobby of mine that I've pretty much mastered over the years: people watching. With nothing better to do, sometimes I'll just watch the humans and come up with stories about their feelings and lives.

Ellie, Corey, Theo, and the other lady all crouch down beside me. Their eyes watering up. *Oh no! Something's wrong.* All four of them with the same dreadful expression. Four pairs of eyes all looking at me sadly. I wish I could ask them what's wrong. I wish I could be there for them.

Ellie says something to Corey and she cautiously extends her arm, her fingers reaching out to me, and I let her pet my head. Her hands are warm and soft as she glides her hand carefully over my head.

She looks into my eyes, and I can see the tears running down her face falling on the dry pavement. And I know what's wrong: *she understands.*

They all have the same look in their grieving eyes. But that look gives me hope because that means they care, someone cares! It means the world to me when people care.

Ellie reaches in, wrapping her arms lovingly around me. I lean into her, what humans call "hug."

Human gestures are a funny thing: shaking hands, waving, hugging, kissing, nodding, shaking their head. Most of them don't make sense, but at the same time, whenever a human hugs me, I feel happy. So maybe some of them don't make sense, but they make us happy.

I swim over to Corey, and she starts to pat my head again, then glides her hand across the top of my head, wrapping her arms around me. It does make me happy. One simple gesture from a human goes a long way.

Cold tears on my head, warm everywhere else. Today she seems a lot different from when I met her before. Before, she was so excited and bright, and now that's gone.

For Tokitae

Chapter 25
Cordelia

I take in a deep breath of the cold, refreshing, salty air, close my eyes, and listen to the sound of spring rain hitting the surface of the calm ocean. This is my home, yet I know a part of me is still with Tokitae back in Miami.

It seems like ages ago that I was last in Miami, now I'm all the way on the other side of country waiting for Janice and Ed.

Their faces light up as they see me walk into the little lighthouse. "Welcome back!" Janice exclaims as she walks over to give me a hug. She squeezes me tightly and rocks back and forth cheerfully.

"How was Miami?" Ed asks as he reaches in to hug us both.

"It was great!" I pause, considering what to

tell them first. "I got to go to the city, and to art galleries, and I went to the beach with some friends!"

"Tell me about these friends," Ed says, shocked… ouch.

"Well, I dunno, they were siblings, and the sister just kinda walked up to me one day and decided that she was gonna show me around the city and we ended up getting really close over those few days," I explain.

"Wow, look at you, making friends left and right," Ed says.

I laugh, "I know. Before you know it, I'm going to be the most popular person around here." Changing the subject, I say, "You know the southern resident who's still in captivity, Lolita, or Tokitae?"

They sigh, and I know my answer. "Yeah," they both reply.

"I think it was the first day in Miami, we went to go see her show. At first, I thought it was really cool and didn't think much of it. Then I got to become friends with Ellie and Theo, whose mom is a trainer there, and I got to meet her in person. I started to realize how small her tank is, so I did some research about her past. I found out that she was captured when she was only four! She was stolen from her family and her home! Other orcas *died* during the capture, and the Southern Residents haven't recovered completely since then!" I exclaim.

"It really is horrible," Janice says. She stares blankly for a moment as if trying to find truth to it all. I know she's already heard Tokitae's story before, but I tell her anyway.

"And she's been kept in horrible conditions! The tank is *way* too small, the fish she's being fed are literally *rotten*, and the water is *contaminated*! It's unfair!" I exclaim. I find myself getting angrier and angrier the more I think about it.

"She's a prisoner even though she's done no crime," Ed says as he shakes his head.

"So, Corey, what are you going to do about it?" Janice asks as she looks down at me from over her glasses.

"I," I pause. "I don't know. Been thinking about it, but I have no idea how I can even help."

My eyes search the room as if to search for the answer, but, of course, there is no answer to be found. "I definitely need to do something, though."

"There have been many organizations trying to bring her home. Lots of people want it, and have been trying for years, but it's difficult to get through to the owners of the Seaquarium," Janice explains.

"Okay, well then who are those organizations? Should I go to them?" I ask.

Ed looks up at me from the papers he was looking over. "You're not going to give this up, will you?" he chuckles.

"Why? Do you think I should?" I ask defensively.

"No, no. Just as long as you know that people aren't always very open-minded to big changes like that," he tells me.

"What do you mean? Why?" I ask.

"Well, you see, Tokitae gets them more money. As long as they're making money off her, then they probably won't want to give her up," he explains.

For Tokitae

"But also think about it with from the owners of Seaquarium's point of view. They probably care about her and love her, and it's hard letting go of someone you love," Janice says. Her voice is calm and still cheerful; she has always tried to look on the bright side of things. I wish I could be more optimistic the same way she is.

"Quite frankly, I don't give a crap about what they think because if they *did* really care about her, then they'd want what's best for her," I say defensively.

"Okay honey, you need to calm down a little," she says.

"Let's go for a walk? We can talk about how you can help then?" Ed suggests.

"Don't you have to work?" I ask.

"Honey, we haven't seen you for over a week, work can wait," Janice says with a laugh.

With that, we step out onto the rocky terrain of the shoreline and start to walk along the line of madrone trees. The air is light and smells fresh after the spring rain, and everything on my left looks green and bright. On my right

For Tokitae

the gray skies gently kiss the calm, vast ocean as rain lightly sprinkles over the landscape.

We walk silently for a little while, our minds all in different places. I still feel hot and riled up from talking and thinking too much about Tokitae, but the light rain cools me down.

The sunlight dances on the oval-shaped leaves of the madrone tree. The outstretched branches twist and turn in all different directions making this tree look whimsical and unreal. It's really one of my favorite kinds of trees because of how unique it looks to me, but maybe that's just my opinion. Its bark is a red-brown color and it peels off and it's thin like paper. Under that bark is a yellow-colored bone of the tree.

The wind blows through those trees, and I close my eyes and listen to the music it makes.

I turn and look to my right, to the glistening surface of the vast ocean. I listen to the sound of the calm water gently hitting the rocky shore that we walk on.

I let out a sigh. "So, what do I do?"

"We should help you reach out to Orca Network, and Friends of Tokitae, and then we

For Tokitae

can go from there," Ed says.

"Yeah, just write them an email explaining who you are, and your connection with Tokitae. Ask them if they have any opportunities that you can take on to help bring her home. Then see what they say," Janice explains.

"That sounds good. Thank you," I say.

The light gray sky has shifted in shades of light pinks and oranges, as the sun begins to set below the horizon.

"I should probably head back," I say.

They nod and walk me back up to the parking lot where my bike is chained. They hug me good-bye and tell me again how happy they are that I'm home.

I grip the handlebars tightly and pedal off. I watch the scenery change around me as I ride on the shoulder of the windy roads. So much has changed since before I left. The grass and trees seem just a little greener, the poppies seem a little brighter, covering more ground.

The ocean, the trees, the flowers, the sunset, it's all perfect. I just want to become a part of it, *become more than I am.*

I glimpse the vast ocean through pockets of trees, and it's already dusk. My whole world has turned to gray. I stop and look out at it for one more moment, the calm waves brushing up against the shoreline. The clouds have cleared up for the sunset, and by now I can see stars very faintly.

I pedal faster as I realize I'm on a time limit before I'll be riding my bike home in the dark.

Janice had texted me a list of people I should email, so, I type in their email addresses and start typing:

Hello,
My name is Cordelia Hart. I am fifteen years old, and I care a lot about the Southern Resident Orcas. I've spent my whole life with them, and I love them each deeply, and I've learned so much from them. I want to try my best to do everything I can to protect them.

Not too long ago, I learned about Tokitae, and

I was lucky enough to get to meet her. I felt this connection to her instantly and after learning more about her story, I decided I need to help her. And that's why I'm reaching out to you.

Do you have any opportunities that I can get on board with to help bring Tokitae home?

Thank you!
-Cordelia

I reread it carefully and hit "send."

Chapter 26
Tokitae

A day passes without seeing Corey, Ellie, or Theo. To my surprise, it rains. It's strange for it to rain in spring. At first it only rains lightly, and I am not threatened by it. Sometimes the storms become really fierce, so much so that it scares me and starts to pull my tank apart. Luckily, it's not that bad, *yet*.

    I tilt my head up and let the warm raindrops hit my face and body, bringing me back to rainy days in the Sound. Although the water and air were much, much cooler and lighter at home, rainy days still used to be my favorite. I would dive down under the surface, letting the echo of each rain drop spread through me, listening to the music of the raindrops hitting the surface of the ocean. We would leap out of the water, flinging ourselves into the air and dive back down in unison.

None of the storms were nearly as bad as they are here, but some days the rain was harsh enough to scare off the salmon, or it was hard to hear the others. Those days were bad. The cold, the not being able to communicate, the hunger…

Suddenly, a gust of harsh winds pushes all the water in my tank back, bringing me with it, into a big wave. The water splashes up and down and up and down, rockily. Lightning darts across the sky and there's a loud crash across the clouds. The rain comes down harder, *harsher.*

Paint breaks off the seats in the stadium, flaking into my pool contaminating it. It's too noisy. It's too loud. Make it stop! Please make it stop! My entire world turns bright for a moment as the light flashes across the sky. Torturous winds push the water up around me.

Creeeeaakkk…

Abruptly, the walls and the concrete start to make very loud noises, making my entire body go tense. My flippers feel numb, my eyes tired but alert, my heart beating so loudly I cannot hear my thoughts. I'm not really able to float at the surface as I usually do, for the water is too monstrous as it splashes over me every time I try to take a breath. The winds, the rain, the water, all working against me, as if I am the enemy, as always.

These are the storms that I fear.

I struggle to swim against the unusual current the wind is creating. I need to find a safe space; I need to find somewhere where the least amount of damage will be done. I can't. I can't make it anywhere. The water is too atrocious, working its way to get to me.

I shut my eyes tightly.

One… two… three… four…

When I open them, I wish for the storm to be over, for all to be well again. Maybe if I wish hard enough, it'll stop. No. Nothing changes. I am still devoured by the antagonizing sounds and winds and rain. There is no counting until the ending, because it is not yet over.

A wave crashes down over me, pushing me under. I let it. While I'm under, I imagine myself under the surface of the Salish Sea, I imagine my family calling out to me gently. I find it in me to sing, hoping that will bring peace to the storm.

The wave brushes me back to the surface, and I gasp, letting go of my breath. I struggle to stay on top of the water, so I bob up and down, being pushed left and right, hoping I won't be pushed into a wall or under the water for too long.

A circular but curved fabric-y material with a rod sticking out of the middle flies through the air, crashing down against the stadium. The crash was loud. So, so, loud. My heart beats faster, louder, my body tenser, making it all the more difficult to stay at the surface.

I sing. I breathe. I struggle. The storm is like a beast, hurling and throwing objects, crying out in rage. Sad, angry, lost. Still brutal towards me and the others here at the park, for we all are unprotected from the elements.

I search my brain thinking of how we would've handled the currents in the real ocean. Come to think of it, I don't believe we had currents and storms nearly as brutal as these. Nevertheless, I know that whatever we would've done, it'd be better than this. At least back then I was not alone.

I get pushed down and pushed to my left again, being held captive under the water. Never being able to find my own way back up to the surface, back up to safety. I'm stuck. Again, I shut my eyes.

One… two… three..

I count to twenty-two, and by the time I reach it, I open my eyes to see the storm is slowly starting to calm down. It's over at last.

For Tokitae

Chapter 27
Cordelia

- Two years later –

I sigh as I finish unpacking all my clothes into my new dresser. I start to wander around this new home. The kitchen is beautiful, with sparkling white granite counter tops, and an abstract light fixture that reminds me of something we would've seen in Miami. Not far from our kitchen is our little humble living room, and on our new couch is my mom. Sprawled across her lap is Bear, our golden retriever black lab mix puppy.

It's a strange feeling leaving the home that you have spent your entire life in. I feel like I'm leaving all my childhood behind, yet I am excited for the new beginning. I tug at my shirt and let out a breath of exhaustion. God, I miss it already.

I glance back at Bear, who has one ear sticking up and the other flopped over, with his head tilted to the side.

"Bear!" I say in a baby voice as I flop down on the couch beside them and start to pet the top of his head playfully.

Mom grabs my free hand and squeezes it tightly, "What's your agenda for today?"

"I don't know yet. I kinda feel like finishing unpacking so I don't have to do it later," I explain.

"Hmm, yeah I think that'll be my plan, too," she says. She runs her hand through my shoulder-length hair. I miss it long, I really do. You could do more things with it, I used to have it layered and it looked really good with my natural waves. Last week, I was sitting in a tree, and I got sap stuck in my hair and I couldn't brush it out! I think this was a very tragic loss for me, clearly.

Mom knows exactly what I'm thinking, "Your hair! I'm not used to it this short!"

"I know it's such a tragic loss; I bet you're having such a hard time dealing with it!" I tease.

For Tokitae

"Of course, I am," she says jokingly. We laugh.

My phone buzzes in my back pocket. I pull it out to find a text from Janice: a link highlighted in blue against her grey/black text bubble. I click on it curiously. A circle with one end chasing the other appears and slowly the link starts to load. The first thing I see is a caption, "It's official: Agreement in place to bring Tokitae home from Miami Seaquarium to Puget Sound!" I reread it again and again. What?! Is this real?! I laugh, smiling with teardrops of happiness trickling down my face.

It seems like there's no way this can be true. It's too good to be true. It's been too long, too tiresome, too emotionally draining. So much hard work, so much hope, so much love showered onto Toki and this issue. And now she is finally getting justice.

She won't die alone after all.

I scroll down and quickly scan over the text, the phrases, "It's official: Agreement in place to bring Tokitae home from Miami Seaquarium to Puget Sound" and, "The movement, once thought impossible, could happen within 18 to 24 months," really stand out to me. They repeat over and over in my head, and my eyes get too cloudy to read anything else.

Tears running down my face, Bear is the first to notice; he tilts his head curiously. "Mom!" I exclaim, "Mom! We did it! We *finally* did it!"

"What? What's wrong?" her words breathy and scared, but once she realizes I'm smiling, she mimics me.

I smile my big, ridiculous goofy grin and show her my phone. "They've made the announcement that there's been an agreement and Toki will come home within the next year or two for sure!"

"Ah! Oh my gosh! Corey!" she gasps, with the same ridiculous goofy grin. She hugs me, squeezing me tightly, rocking side-to-side.

I cry more into her shoulder, and she hugs me tighter. "I can't believe it's finally happening!" I sob.

She whispers, "I know, I know."

Like I said, a lot has changed over the past

two years, especially with Tokitae. Ellie, Theo, and I followed through with trying our best to help bring Tokitae home, although I know it was hard for both of them.

    I worked with organizations, Orca Network, and Friends of Tokitae, to spread the word, petition, protest, and hold events in honor of her capture. I worked hard creating and handing fliers to everyone, talking non-stop about it, and telling others to do the same. I started my own blog about her and her past, and the tireless efforts made to bring her home. I signed - and forced everyone I knew to sign - petitions that came across my way. Every summer for the past few years, on August 8th, mom and I travel to Penn Cove on Whidbey Island to participate in this huge event to honor Toki and remember her capture. Everything I did, I did it for her.

    My mom got offered a second interview for that job she tried to get, so, we ended up traveling back to Miami, and I got to see my friends again. There, we held a peaceful protest outside of the Seaquarium for Toki. Mom decided not to take the job because she just couldn't leave Friday Harbor and take me from my orcas. If she left, it would also mean her gallery business would have to close.

Speaking of my friends, they too have been advocating for Tokitae, which is great to have people in Miami and better having people in the Seaquarium who have more insight about the issue there. They tried to raise awareness inside the aquarium, and they even tried to confront the owners about it… of course nobody listened.

I still remember the first time I found out about this issue. I remember it very clearly, the way the light glistened through our window, and the way I felt like I wanted to throw a brick through that window because of how mad I was that this was happening. I remember the fear of how I was going to tell my friends.

We've come a long way. I can't imagine how the people who were fighting for her for over twenty years must feel. I think back to the fear that I felt to tell Ellie and Theo, but now, I'm so, so excited to tell them this news.

"I can't believe it!" I sob.

"Honey, I'm so happy for you!" she says.

For Tokitae

"I'm so happy for Toki!" I close my eyes and inhale slowly. I think back to her, how lifeless she would float there, how meaningless everything must have been to her. At the same time, it wasn't at all meaningless. She was put through so much, yet she still had held on to hope, and that is the most meaningful thing I have ever heard.

Now, whenever something seems to go wrong in *my* life, I think back to the way she had lost everything; I think back to how meaningless her life was after that, but she was so, *so* strong. She's lost everything and still she goes on, she doesn't give up hope.

I remember the last day of our trip. Right before we were leaving, I said good-bye to her. I remember so vividly the way she looked into my eyes, she looked so hopeful, and I wanted her to be happy so, so badly. I still do.

Now, two years later, after fighting so hard for her, that happiness finally is going to happen! She won't have to be hopeful anymore because she'll be getting her life back!

I take in deep breaths, and smile. I focus on

my smile not my tears, and I wipe the dampness from my eyes. I stand back up, and head back to my room as I call Ellie.

"Hello?" she answers.

"Ellie! Oh my G-"she cuts me off.

"Did you see it, too!?" I have to move my phone away from my ear a little because of how loud and how excited she is.

"Yes!" I exclaim.

"I'm so happy for her!" The radiant joy running through her carries even across the phone. Her happiness is contagious as it always seems to be.

"Me too! Are you with her anytime soon?" I ask.

"Well, I don't think I told you. I *finally* convinced my mom to quit her job, so she wasn't supporting the Seaquarium! I still get to see her though, thankfully, because Theo and I get special VIP access," she flexes.

"Ellie! That's great!" Everything seems to be going right.

After we hang up, I try to calm myself, but I'm just too excited. This must be the best day

I've had in a long time. So, I open up my email and write:

Hello,

I'm so excited to hear about this amazing news that we finally have permission to bring Tokitae home. I am so thrilled to hear this, and I am so, so happy for her!
I understand that there is still a long and bumpy road ahead of us, but I would like to help in any way I can along this process. Please let me know what I can do.

Again, I am so happy for her!

Thank you so much!

-Cordelia

Chapter 28
Tokitae

The entire atmosphere of the aquarium has seemed different in the past few days. Although it seems as if the exhaustion has been playing a game of tag with me - one moment I'll be fine, the next, it catches up to me.

My mom used to tell me that despite the conditions of that day, I should be overly grateful for every day I have. I still hold that to be the truth. When I start feeling this way, I dig into my memories and remember my time with my family in the wild, free waters.

I remember diving down in a blanket of green-gray water through the passage on one particularly sad day, yet that day was so filled with hope. The cool spring mist gently spraying our dorsal fins and backs as we surfaced, the water fighting against our bodies. The salmon were a little too fast that day and the current was a little too strong.

Despite that, the earth still provided for us. We still had the sea, and the salmon, and each other, and that was enough of a reason to be grateful. She would tell me to always find things to be grateful for.

Now that I've lost all those things, I am grateful for the memories. I am grateful for the limited years I had at home. At the aquarium, I am grateful for the people, both the ones who I get to inspire and those who inspire me.

Speaking of people, in recent months, Ellie and Theo seem much, much happier! They even speak of my return home!

It was a scorching hot day, yet they still came in the sun. Ellie with her usual enthusiasm and Theo with more than usual. They almost skipped up to me with beautiful, smiling faces.

"Tokitae!" I love hearing that name being used for me now. It feels as if the mask of Lolita is finally being taken off.

"We have some exciting news for you!" she

For Tokitae

told me. Her face said it all: this would be the moment I was waiting for, this would be it.

That night was restless. All I did was gaze up at the schools of fish in the sky, listening to the gentle waves off in the distance. Listening to the calls of my family far, far away pulled out of a memory.

The only thoughts that filled my mind were that very soon I'd be gazing at the stars alongside them. I think I've waited long enough.

In the months since the news, I have been poked and prodded non-stop by vets, and have had many men in fine clothing that looked as if they were going to overheat wearing it, stare at me discussing what they'll end up doing with me. Neither of these things are necessarily enjoyable, but if it's what it takes for me to come home, it's worth it.

I'm ready to go home.

For Tokitae

Chapter 29
Cordelia

- August –

The immense line of dark blue expands in front of me. The sun catches the delicate ripples and small waves that glisten so beautifully it doesn't seem real. There's something about the lighthouse in the summer, maybe it's the warm sun, the chatter of people around, the excitement for the whales, the calm winds, the salty air. It makes it seems as if all your worries can't touch you here.

It's strange to think that three summers ago my mom wouldn't have any interest in sitting here waiting for four hours with me. She would've been too busy with making money or fighting with my dad - things we don't worry about anymore.

For Tokitae

"We've been here for *so* long," mom complains. Maybe she's not quite at the point of waiting four hours yet, but at least it's something.

"And? You just have to be at the right place at the right time. So, if you put yourself in that place all the time, your destined to see them at some point," I explain.

"So, you're going to live your life staring at the ocean?" she asks with a smirk.

"Mhm. Sounds like the dream life right there," I say.

I laugh to myself thinking about how crazy it is that maybe that statement is somewhat true. In what seems like a hopeless world, being here, staring at the ocean, I find hope. I wonder how Toki did it so far from the Salish Sea? I wonder what gave her hope?

I will say, one thing that doesn't give me hope is the fact that I've come here almost single every day this summer, and last spring, but the SRKWs haven't been here very much at all. I don't know what's going on. Each year, our salmon population decreases, and if we keep this up, we won't have salmon anymore, and that means no orcas. I fear that that "no salmon, no orcas" time is going to come very soon.

"Are you bored?" I ask.

"Yes," she doesn't even hesitate to answer.

"Do you wanna go see Janice and Ed?" I ask.

"They're still here, too?" she asks.

"Should be. They work here," I point out.

It's a warm August afternoon, the park is pretty crowded, like it always is on most summer afternoons. Everyone talks excitedly, hoping that a whale will break through the surface of the water at any moment.

Janice and Ed's faces light up when they see me, as they always do. "Hello!"

"Hey," I greet them.

"What's new with Tokitae?" They ask this almost every time I see them.

Even a lot has happened with Tokitae since we found out our plan was permitted last March. And so much has happened over the last two years.

Last year, the Miami Seaquarium got new owners, and they really helped Toki. They

For Tokitae

retired her, meaning that they announced that she wouldn't be staging shows under the agreement with federal regulators. Under the Dolphin Company's new license with the U.S. Department of Agriculture, Tokitae and her companion, a white-sided dolphin, stopped being exhibited. Because of Toki's retirement, her health has begun to improve, and the new owners of the Miami Seaquarium told a Lummi Elder that they would support bringing Toki home if certain health standards were met.

Last March was when we got the announcement that the Seaquarium was on board with bringing Toki back home. The Miami Seaquarium and the Friends of Lolita Foundation have a "formal and binding agreement" to begin this process. She will be coming home now within 18-24 months! And I can't wait! Last May, there was another announcement from Miami and Friends of Lolita that Tokitae is in good condition and our plans have been moving forward.

So, what's the plan? Toki has spent most of her life in captivity; therefore, we can't just throw her back in the ocean and say, "good luck!" But she was a juvenile when she was captured, meaning she knows the language, hunting strategies, and the ways of the SRKWs. So, Orca Network and Friends of Lolita have made this plan to bring Tokitae back and put her in a sea-pen, which is a closed off place in the Salish Sea. There, she would get 24/7 care from people, but she would still be able to be in the ocean. She'd be getting her freedom back one step at a time.

Now, what have I been doing? Along with following her story and staying in touch with the people who are more involved, I have been writing blog posts about it, writing lots of thank you emails to everyone who's made this possible and trying to get more on board with it all… although that's hard to do since this is all so new.

"I just can't believe this is happening!" I exclaim. Lately, I've been smiling so much my face is beginning to hurt.

But not Janice… Janice looks like she's blinking back tears. She looks up and she bites her lip; her eyes dart up and down me. Uh-oh, what'd I say?

For Tokitae

"I remember when we saw Tahlequah," she pauses. That was one of the hardest days of my life, and it was very emotional for both of us. "Honey, we were so hopeless, it was so, *so* heartbreaking seeing that dead calf. And seeing the way Tahlequah didn't let go for days and days. After that, you just seemed so off… I felt like you were fading from us and there wasn't anything we can do. This whale has brought you back to us."

She pulls me into a hug and squeezes me tightly like the day she did when I came back home from Miami. I realize, she's right. I think I kind of lost myself for a while there. I was caught up in this web of overwhelming, constant stress about my parents. Tokitae helped me find myself again and break free of that web.

"Think about Tokitae's journey, though. This is *huge* for her," I say.

"I know! And I'm so happy for her!" she exclaims.

"Me, too!" I reply.

Mom grabs my hand, and squeezes it, teary eyed she says, "I think Tokitae has brought us closer together, too."

"Definitely," I smile. We look at each other knowingly.

Suddenly, outside I hear screaming and commotion. We all rush out with one thought on our minds... orcas!

Chapter 30
Cordelia

They are here! This is the first time I've seen them all summer long! The world goes silent and everything stops as they break the surface, exhaling abruptly with a *pffft* sound.

I get this happy feeling in my heart as I notice Ocean Sun L25 surfacing. We believe that she is Tokitae's mother because, even though it's hard to know with these things, she used to swim with Toki when she was young. I can see her beautiful white swirly saddle patch as she gracefully surfaces. Seeing her is a rare occasion because she doesn't typically travel with any of the pods. Some believe that this is because she is still searching for Toki - I think she is. Maybe she knows that Toki will be returning home soon!

What I see next takes my breath away. I

For Tokitae

can't believe my eyes! I gasp as I notice the two new L pod calves swimming close to her side, this is the first time I've seen them! They porpoise together, moving in unison, breathing in unison, co-existing together, depending on each other. I can't begin to describe how beautiful it is.

This indescribable feeling of peace, and comfort fills me as I breathe in. As I breathe out, I let go. I let go of everything that's holding me back, and I feel light and free.

I feel like I could blow away in these winds and dance through the outstretched leaves of the trees. I watch as the orcas move, they porpoise, breach, spy-hop; I don't know where to look, they're everywhere. They're all so deeply connected to one another, even just watching them you can almost feel the love they have for one another.

They are so beautiful.

They are so majestic.

Truly breathtaking.

The L pod babies are so small and adorable. As they surface, I can see their underside is still that adorable yellow-orange color that they haven't yet grown out of.

Mom squeezes my hand lovingly, and I look over to see her teary-eyed once again. This is the first time in *years* that she has seen them in the wild. I don't remember the last time I saw the Southern Residents with her, that's how long it's been.

I began to get teary-eyed, too, as I always do while watching the whales.

Mom leans in and whispers, "They're pretty incredible," she gasps and squeezes my hand tighter. "I love you."

So, here I am, sitting side-by-side with my mom, watching the oldest orca and the two youngest, and she told me that she loved me for the first time in the longest time that I can remember. And Tokitae, the "person" who has helped us find ourselves again, is finally going to get reunited with her mom, like my mom and I have.

We're all so hopeful.

I close my eyes, and listen. I hear the water crashing against the rocky shore, I hear people talking hushed, but still excitedly off in the distance. I hear the exhaling of the orcas as they surface, and wind musically flowing through the madrone trees. And everything is okay.

Everything is perfect.

I open my eyes, to see that the number of whales has multiplied! The K pod is now swimming along with the Ls, and the J16s have arrived now, too. *Are we going to get a superpod?!*

I let out a sigh and stretch out my arms as I let the wind run through my fingertips.

By the next hour, all seventy-five individuals have arrived. Something is different about today. I feel different; peaceful, maybe? I think that's because I'm here, and so are they. Although…the pods don't usually gather except for births and deaths, and no orcas have died recently that we know of.

"Janice? Ed?" I turn to them and talk quietly.

They turn to me and wait for me to say something.

"Why are they all here? Was there another calf? Or death?" I ask.

They both look confused, "Hmm, I don't

know."

That's when it dawns on me, they know Tokitae will come home soon. And that is a reason for hope.

Our gaze doesn't leave the whales for a millisecond. We see Blackberry J-27 launch himself out of the water and crash down again freely, and a K pod orca stick her head out of the water and bob it back down.

I probably look like the Grinch again, with that smile literally coming off of my face... oh well.

The sudden ringing of my phone interrupts the peace and quietness of the whales. Should I ignore it? It's probably a scam anyway. Just to make sure, I pull it out of my pocket; it's Ellie.

I answer quietly, "Hello?"

"Corey!" she gasps, sobbing. I start to panic; what's wrong with her?

"What?! What's wrong?" I ask, not caring about my volume anymore.

"It's Tokitae!" she says, choking on her words.

"She's... she's dead!" Her voice is dry and

empty, like every last bit of her has disappeared.

It takes me a second to process what she just said. It can't be true. I know it's not true because she's coming home. They just said she *is* healthy.

"No! NO! You are a liar! She's - she's..." Everyone turns to look at me. I don't care. I let out a sob, knowing that she's telling the truth. "She's healthy. She's coming home though... Don't lie to me."

I hear Ellie sobbing on the other end of the phone. My entire body goes sharp, my legs give out and I fall onto my knees. My head falls into my hands, sobbing. This can't be true.

Yet it is.

"I don't know what happened. She must have been sick." Her voice is drained and gloomy.

I don't want to believe it.

Despite that I choke out, "I believe you."

I hang up, dropping my phone on the rocks. I collapse into my mom's arms and I sob, breathing heavily, choking on my own tears.

"What's wrong? Corey? Talk to us!" Janice

and Ed and my mom all try to get me to say something.

When I finally catch my breath, I mutter, "Toki... Toki *died.*"

They all gasp in horror. Janice and Ed fall into each other, both with tears running down their faces and my mom holds me tight to her. I can feel her shaking.

It doesn't feel real. Only a moment ago, we were all excited for her return home - *that was real.*

It's not fair! What were we thinking? Why did we let it go on as long as we did? She meant so much to so many people, and now everything she taught us will be lost. It will all be for nothing.

I feel sick to my stomach, with every sob I feel as if I could throw up. My limbs feel numb and my head is pounding.

Just an hour ago, we were living in the hope and in belief that she'd return home. She was healthy a month ago, what happened?

"It's not fair..." I cry.

Chapter 31
Tokitae

I know it's coming, but that's okay. It's been a peaceful day today, not very many people around, left to listen to my own thoughts. The sun hits the water of my tank, capturing it in its glow, warming my body. It's sunny out, *warm* but not hot. A few fluffy clouds are spread out across the blue sky. The world *is* beautiful, even here from my tank.

I think back to those early days, how lucky I was. I really did have it all, my family, the sea, my freedom. Even in my captive life, I still have those memories. I still have that will to live for those memories. I still have the chance to give others happy memories.

These last few days have been harder and harder. I don't know how much longer I will be able to wait. I am okay with that. I feel at peace knowing that my life *did* mean something, and my spirit will go on.

I believe that there is beauty in death, too. I know that I was more than just a sad story. I was more than just a living injustice, and I am thankful for that. There is beauty knowing that I will get my closure, and my spirit will be home again. I sense the pods gathering today at Lime Kiln to welcome me home.

As I take my last breaths, I sing my mother's song.

For Tokitae

Chapter 32
Cordelia

I shut my eyes tightly and remember the first time I saw her. It was two years ago, the first time I went to Miami. I remember so vividly the way she stared into my eyes, calling for help. I remember the way her smooth skin felt as I embraced her before leaving. What I remember the clearest though is the connection I had instantly. But I also remember the anger and remorse I felt about her past and the injustice that we had put her through. I remember the way she had so much hope. She lost everything, but kept persevering, and hoped for her resolution that would never come.

    I remember when we were promised that her long awaited return home would happen within 18 months. I remember the joy we all experienced that day. All the long nights of feeling sad about her life, all the excitement of her return home. It felt good to do something good, something truly worthwhile.

Now it's gone.

Now *she's* gone.

This wasn't the ending that we wanted; this wasn't the life she deserved... but I feel at peace knowing she has been reunited with these orcas right in front of my eyes.

Although we are all in so much pain right now, I know it won't last forever. What *will* last forever is her spirit. We all know that she is swimming with the 70+ orcas in front of me.

I scan the water to find Ocean Sun, and I see her with the calves, and I wonder: is Tokitae swimming beside her? I get this sudden feeling deep down *that she is*.

What am I supposed to do now that she's gone? I'm going to miss her so, so much. But part of me knows that I won't have to miss her, because I will still see her. I'll see her when I gaze out into the open ocean, for I'll be reminded of her and all she has taught me. I'll be reminded of her when I feel the warm sun fill me. I'll be reminded of her whenever I feel the wind through my outstretched fingertips.

She's finally free.

For Tokitae

Epilogue

As I sit along the shore, watching cedar boughs and flowers float away in the water, I know I'll never forget her. Whenever I feel hopeless, I'll think about her, and then I won't have to feel hopeless anymore. I watch as the cedar boughs gently roll in the waves and as a single rose washes up to shore. It lands in the shiny pebbles near my feet. I pick it up, examining the soft, red petals dripping with salt water and my memories rush over me like the waves.

 I remember when I first started to learn about her story. The phrase, "don't let her die alone" used to repeat in my head. In the end, I don't think she did, because so many people loved her and cared about her, and that counts for something.

 Her life isn't fair; she deserved so much better.

For Tokitae

Don't let her death be in vain…that is the new mantra that repeats in my head. We need to come together, like the Salish Sea orcas, and we need to fight for her family, and fight for our ecosystem.

A lot has changed since I first began my story. With Toki's help, I found myself and I found my purpose. What I've realized through it all is, this isn't *just* my story. This is *not* just the story of Cordelia Hart and Tokitae, this is a story of *hope*.

Note From the Author

Dear readers,

    Thank you for reading *For Tokitae*. I started writing this book before her death in hopes that it would help spread the word about the injustices she was facing, and it would inspire us to take action for her return home. Unfortunately, that is not the ending we got. I hope that this book will remind us all of the costs of human greed for the purpose of entertainment, and the sacrifices that she and her family were forced to make. Most of all, I hope that this book helps us remember all that Tokitae symbolized, and this will give us a way to honor her and let her story be told. I believe that hers is a very important and very impactful story, and that we can all learn something from Tokitae. I know that there are many better ways to tell this story, but I did it the best that I can.

    My goal while writing this book was to relate the struggles of a lost teenager to an amazing orca who horrifically lost it all, and to

For Tokitae

have Toki help Corey find herself through the novel. I chose the name Cordelia (Corey) because it means heart and guardian of the sea.

We should all try to be a little bit more like Tokitae, because despite the bitter conditions and her brutal backstory, she remained hopeful and optimistic. (The words "bitter" and "brutal" are very much an understatement when it comes to describing her life and the conditions in which she was forced to live.)

I worry that by the time we start to make changes for a better environment, it will be too late. Much like by the time they agreed to free Tokitae it had been much too late.

Like Corey says, "Don't let her death be in vain." Now, is the time to do as much as possible to protect her family, our ecosystem, and the suffering world that we live in.

Over the next few pages, you'll find resources to help guide you in making an impact for good. This book is realistic fiction, meaning parts of it were true and parts were not. For instance, all human characters are fictional, as are their stories, feelings, and experiences, but

For Tokitae

Tokitae and her story were based on reality. The next few pages will also go over the facts of Tokitae's story and that of her family.

For Tokitae

Facts:

Tokitae is known to the Lummi Nation as Sk'aliCh'elh-tenaut. On August 8th, 1970, a horrific capture took place. A group of whale herders rounded up a pod of the Southern Resident Killer Whales in the Puget Sound of Washington State. They used aircraft, speed boats, and explosives to force the orcas into Penn Cove, separating the adults from the juvenile orcas. The young whales were the main target because they were highly desired by aquariums. Although the adults were free to leave and swim away, they refused to and cried as they watched their infants being taken from them. The capture stole the lives of one adult and four infant orcas. To keep the deaths hidden from the public, the whale herders slit the bellies of the infants to sink them to the bottom of the Salish Sea. This capture led to the loss of an entire generation of Southern Resident Orcas.

 The SRKWs do not leave their mothers

For Tokitae

their *entire* lives. The orca that is thought to be Tokitae's mother, L25, Ocean Sun, is approximately ninety years-old and many believe she still searches for her. To this day, none of the Southern Residents have returned to Penn Cove. This only proves how much the capture impacted them and how deeply they feel for their families.

On September 24th, 1970, at only four-years-old, Tokitae was sold to the Miami Seaquarium. She spent the next 53 years of her life there under the name of Lolita, where she was forced to do tricks and perform.

She lived in unbearable conditions. She was not protected by the elements, nor was she in a clean, safe environment. The fish that she fed were rotten, the water in her tank was contaminated, and the size of the tank was illegally small. Tokitae's tank violated the APHIS standards for size requirements. She was about 21 feet long, and 7,000 pounds. The guidelines for an orca her size is *at least* 48 feet wide in both directions, but her tank was only 35 feet wide from the front to the barrier, and only 20 feet deep in the deepest section.

Ken Balcomb from Center for Whale Research and Howard Garrett from Orca Network had a plan to bring her home. She would be transported from Miami to a cove off of San Juan Islands by cargo plane. It would be unreasonable to throw her back into the ocean after being in captivity for so long, and say, "good luck!" so, she would have been going through a rehabilitation process. She would have lived in a sea pen, under constant human care. The goal was that over time she could have started to pick up the ways of the Salish Sea and possibly have been able to swim free with her family again.

The following is the timeline for the major announcements that promised her return home: In August of 2021 the Dolphin Company purchased the Miami Seaquarium. As part of the agreement, they promised her retirement. She then stopped performing. The following month brought the USDA Report on Tokitae's health, revealing the horrid conditions she was living under. Finally, on March 30th, 2023, the day that so many had been waiting for, was the announcement that she would *finally* return home.

The owners of the Miami Seaquarium made a "formal and binding agreement" with Friends of Lolita to begin the process of her long-awaited return home. James Irsay, the owner of the NFL's Indianapolis Colts, made a very generous contribution, covering all the expenses the plan would take.

This was the moment that so, so many had been waiting for. Organizations such as the Friends of Lolita, Orca Network, Center for Whale Research, Save Lolita, and many others had been advocating for this moment for *years*. Many indigenous communities, including the Lummi Nation, had fought for this for *years*. Many, many individuals across the globe had longed for this moment for *years*. There were many tireless efforts made for her return home, for what was right. March 30th, 2023 was the day that everyone thought we had just won the battle.

For Tokitae

Tokitae died on August 18th, 2023. She was 57 years old. Fifty-three of those years had been spent away from her home. Can you imagine that? Fifty-three years away from home. Fifty-three years away from her family. Fifty-three years of being mistreated. And for what?

August 18th, 2023 was the day our hearts broke. We were so close to the happy ending we had been promised. Empty words and forgotten promises still held tremendous meaning.

How Tokitae Affected Real People

Much like Corey, when I first heard about Tokitae, I felt instant anger, and I wanted to do something. I know this was the same for many, *many* others who should be talking about this instead of me right now. I started following her story, writing this novel, and telling everyone. I remember how heartbroken I was the day I found out she died. The thing is, I only knew her story for around a year, so many others had been following and advocating for her for so many more years. There were people across the globe grieving her loss.

    I was privileged enough to work with the Orca Network's amazing education coordinator, Cindy Hanson, and media coordinator, Kaarina Makowski, to hold a memorial in the South Sound at the Thea Foss Waterway in Tacoma - thank you to Julia Berg for helping with the venue.

That was my first time public speaking. All morning I was terrified because of two reasons; one, public speaking is scary for everyone; two, this was a heavily emotional topic. At the beginning of the memorial, I began talking to people, and I was *amazed* by how many lives Tokitae touched. All my nervousness of public speaking faded away after hearing stories about how she affected people's lives.

Tokitae was loved not only widely, but so deeply. There were people at the memorial who had known her their *entire* lives. I was listening to stories of someone who had visited her as a child and saw her and started to make a scene about it in the middle of the aquarium. I was listening to stories of how she had changed and even saved lives. I was talking to people who had struggled with the grief and anger for Tokitae for *years*. I was talking to people who had advocated for her for decades only to have this as the ending. There were people who traveled across the country to honor her life. She meant that much.

She symbolized so much hope, and

optimism about the future. She suffered from losing *everything,* but she still kept going for fifty-three more years. If there's one thing that I want you to get from this book, it's that we should all adopt Tokitae's attitude about the future if we want there to be change.

At the same time, we, as human beings, should feel ashamed of what we have done to the environment and poor animals like Tokitae. We should *not* let the years of pain be forgotten. We should *not* let this be the end. Now, we must take action to protect her family, advocate for animal rights and restore our ecosystems.

Don't let her death be in vain.

For Tokitae

What can I do?

The Southern Resident orcas have three main threats. One threat is pollution. When it rains, the stormwater collects on the pavement then goes down the drains into the streams and rivers leading out to the ocean. With it comes the harmful chemicals from the land. This process is called stormwater runoff.

Another threat to orcas is lack of food. Environmental issues such as climate change, stormwater runoff, and dams are killing off the salmon. According to the EPA, Salish Sea Chinook salmon populations are down 60% since tracking salmon abundance in 1984. One hundred thirty-seven different species rely on salmon for survival. Salmon are our keystone species; without them our ecosystem will begin to unravel.

The last threat is boat vessel noise. Because of the sonic noise that boat vessels produce, it makes hunting and communication hard for the SRKWs.

To help Tokitae's family, you can plant trees and do restoration work, follow Whale Wise requirements while boating, and advocate for the removal of the dams on Snake River in Washington.

Planting trees and doing restoration work helps because it acts as a natural filtration system for stormwater runoff. Planting native plants helps maintain a healthy ecosystem along streams and rivers. Following Whale Wise requirements means giving the whales the space they need to thrive.

Sources and additional information:

- Save Lolita (I highly recommend looking at this site): https://www.savelolita.org/
- USDA report: https://www.nbcmiami.com/news/local/usda-report-details-violations-and-animal-safety-concerns-at-miami-seaquarium/3150773/#:~:text=The%20remains%20of%20the%20orca,that%20her%20tank%20was%20dirty.
- Tokitae's life timeline: https://www.king5.com/article/news/local/timeline-tokitae-efforts-bring-her-home/281-6c53a7c1-ced9-4805-980d-57daa0e30431
- One Tree Planted SRKW video (I highly recommend watching): https://www.youtube.com/watch?v=E7aZQ6o9-T4
- Orca Netwok (Please support!): https://www.orcanetwork.org/
- Whale Museum (Please support!): https://whalemuseum.org/
- South Sound memorial for Tokitae: https://www.youtube.com/live/C9-uTV7ATqQ?si=1UClwEFKCfl6qQWP
- Jane Goodall Institute Roots and Shoots: (create your own, or join a local group!) https://rootsandshoots.org/
- Becci Crowe (Inspiring conservationist, artist and public speaker): https://www.becci.com/

About the Author

I started writing this book when I was thirteen-years old; when I first heard about Tokitae. It took me over a year to write and had a much different ending than I had expected and hoped for.

My passion for wildlife and environmental issues started long before that. When I was around seven years old, I heard about Dr. Jane Goodall and decided that I wanted to be just like her and save the earth. My friends and I started a group where we would go to the library at recess and read about different plants and animals. We called it "Nature Kids." When I began middle school, I was lucky enough to start an Environmental Club there. The focus of the Environmental Club is to bring awareness and create opportunities for environmental conservation and restoration projects in our school and with the community.

At age eleven, I first learned about the Southern Residents. After hearing Tahlequah's story, I was immediately fascinated by these amazing creatures. For my birthday that year, I "adopted" Tahlequah through the Whale Museum. On a family trip to Friday Harbor, I saw the J and L pods for the first time. My parents waited with me for eight hours, just staring at the sea waiting for whales to arrive. Occasionally, we would make small talk with others who visited Lime Kiln. At some point, we were talking to a woman who had traveled from Texas and backpacked across the peninsula for days. She told us about her experiences with the orcas and what they meant to her. That was the first time I heard about Tokitae.

Like many others, I felt angry and sad when learning about her life. The following months, I started doing as much as I could to help including writing this story. After her death, I was devastated, just like Cordelia.

I partnered with the Orca Network to hold a memorial in honor of Tolitae's life. Even after all that had ended, I decided to continue my novel to keep her story alive.

I continue my environmental work as a certified steward and volunteer with Metro Parks. I have taken many training sessions with the Whale Museum and the Orca Network to educate myself on the Puget Sound ecosystem.

Through my environmental efforts, I even got the opportunity to meet with my idol, Dr. Jane Goodall! That experience changed my life.

I plan to move forward to create a network of individuals who care tremendously about the planet. With that network, we can create opportunities for community conservation projects through *Roots & Shoots*. Together we can make a difference!

Together we can change the world!

For Tokitae

Special thanks to:

Suzanne Sarachman and Tara Chase, for the countless hours they have dedicated to our Environmental Club, and for the endless support and motivation.

Mallory Schramm, for helping edit my novel and for all of her excitement for me.

Hannah Newell, for her support and encouragement with running our club, and for all of the work she has done in the community.

Sean Arent and Kevin Johnson, for all of the work they have done at Swan Creek, and all the support with becoming a steward.

Cindy Hansen, for helping me hold a memorial for Tokitae and for all of her endless motivation in saving the amazing Southern Resident Orcas and their ecosystem.

My parents, for always loving and supporting me.

Made in the USA
Columbia, SC
05 August 2024

fa614685-a100-44a7-a9cf-ca549ddaf812R02